Ghost Voyages II

The Matthew

Ghost Voyages II

The Matthew

CORA TAYLOR

Edited by Geoffrey Ursell.
Cover painting by Yves Noblet.
Cover and book design by Duncan Campbell.
Printed and bound in Canada by Transcontinental Printing

Stamps reproduced courtesy Canada Post Corporation.

National Library of Canada Cataloguing in Publication Data

Taylor, Cora, 1936-
Ghost voyages II

ISBN 1-55050-198-4

1. Cabot, John, d. 1498?—Juvenile fiction. I. Title.
PS8589.A883G56 2002 jC813'.54 C2002-910312-6
PZ7.T21235Gho 2002

10 9 8 7 6 5 4 3 2 1

COTEAU BOOKS
401-2206 Dewdney Ave.
Regina, Saskatchewan
Canada S4R 1H3

AVAILABLE IN THE US FROM
General Distribution Services
4500 Witmer Industrial Estates
Niagara Falls, NY 14305-1386

The publisher gratefully acknowledges the financial assistance of the Saskatchewan Arts Board, the Canada Council for the Arts, including the Millennium Arts Fund, the Government of Canada through the Book Publishing Industry Development Program (BPIDP), and the City of Regina Arts Commission, for its publishing program.

The Canada Council for the Arts
Le Conseil des Arts du Canada

Canada

This book is lovingly dedicated
to my grandsons
Justin Livingston,
Harrison Taylor,
Calvin Taylor,
Alexander Mogg,
and, of course, Jeremy and Charlie
who were there the first time.

1.

IF EVER JEREMY WANTED TO ESCAPE IT WAS NOW.

Had it been a week since the letter came? No, it wasn't even that long. It had come on Tuesday and today was only Saturday.

Yes, it had been Tuesday. He'd picked it out of the mailbox when he came home from soccer practice. He remembered because he headed straight for the kitchen. He was starving – as usual. That was why the letter had ended up on the kitchen table with some flyers and other junk mail and his mum hadn't noticed it right away.

In fact, he remembered, she'd almost scooped the whole pile of papers into the garbage.

He lay on his bed staring miserably at the ceiling, wishing she'd done just that. He could hear her in the kitchen just down the hall angrily slamming dishes into the dishwasher.

Things were so miserable that it even made him wish

it wasn't summer holidays – he'd actually have welcomed escaping to school.

First the move. He kept telling himself it could have been worse. After all they'd only moved to the house next door. Mrs. Plunkett's bungalow had gone up for sale when she'd decided to move to Calgary to live with her daughter. So there *had* been a bright spot this summer – no more of the Dread Plunkett babysitting. And except for the fact that he'd had to pack all his stuff and lug it next door, he had a bigger room now. He didn't mind that it was a smaller house. They still had all the main stuff – kitchen, bathroom, living room, and two bedrooms – it was just that now it was all on one floor. That was okay with him. And for awhile his mother had been pretty cheerful. A smaller house meant lower mortgage payments.

But then his best friend, Charlie had gone to the Coast vacationing on Vancouver Island with his parents, while Jeremy was stuck here in Edmonton. Mum had decided they couldn't afford a holiday this year. He'd been unhappy about that at the time. No holiday and no Charlie to hang out with. By the time Charlie got back there would just be a few days before school.

He hadn't known when he was well off. That was B.L. Before the Letter. Ever since the letter, life had become a hundred times worse. Since then his mother was either furious or crying in her room.

And for the first day or two he hadn't known why.

One minute she'd be tearfully giving him a bone-crushing hug, the next she was staring at him as if he was somehow the cause of all the trouble.

"What's the matter, Mum?" he'd ask. But she'd just say "Never mind," or "I'll tell you later," and start slamming things around or run to her room crying.

If it hadn't been for yesterday's phone call from Aunt Wendy, he probably wouldn't have a clue even now.

"So, how are things in your part of the world, kiddo!" Aunt Wendy's voice was bright and cheerful and fun. Just like her.

Jeremy didn't even try to pretend. "Awful," he said. "Couldn't be worse! Mum's in a bad mood and I don't know why. She's..."

Jeremy hadn't realized his mother was there until she snatched the phone out of his hand. He could just hear Aunt Wendy asking something but couldn't make out what. Easy to guess though – she was asking what was wrong. He didn't get a chance to say anything. His mother gave him a hard shove and pointed to his room.

"Private conversation," she whispered fiercely as she pulled the cord on the receiver as far as it would go and disappeared around the corner into the living room.

He didn't argue. He went down the hall but he didn't go to his room. He went into the bathroom, flushed the toilet and slithered silently into his mother's room to pick up the extension, hoping his mother wouldn't hear the click.

He could hear Aunt Wendy's anxious voice. "Sandy,

what's the matter? The kid sounds really upset."

Mum's voice was shrill. "He's upset! He doesn't even know what upset is...." Now her voice was tearful. "Do you know what Darrin has done?"

"No, but you'd better calm down and tell me!"

"He's starting court proceedings to get custody of Jeremy!"

His mother's voice rose again. Jeremy knew he should put the phone down and bolt to his room. If his mother caught him disobeying there'd be serious trouble. Besides if he left the door ajar he could probably hear her anyway she was yelling so loud. But he couldn't. He couldn't move. He just stood there paralyzed. Listening.

"Six years and he hasn't even seen the child and now, suddenly, out of the blue, he wants custody!"

The last word was almost a scream. Jeremy pulled the receiver away from his ear. He didn't want to hear any more. He hung up the phone as quietly as he could and walked woodenly to his room, closed the door and lay down on his bed, staring at the ceiling.

That's what he was doing now. He'd been doing a lot of that since the phone call.

He hadn't seen his dad since he was four years old. It had been just Mum and him ever since.

At first he'd missed Dad, but really he hadn't been around much the year or so before he left. Jeremy was in daycare and then playschool, and what with starting grade one and then moving because his mother couldn't afford to keep that house, there were just so many changes to cope with, not having a father around hadn't been that big a change.

And at first there'd been Grandad. Jeremy had missed him more when he died than he had his dad.

He got up and walked slowly over to his desk. Thinking of Grandad reminded him of something. Escaping.

He hadn't thought of the stamps since his birthday. Something had happened when he turned ten, so the stamps didn't work magic any more. He fished in his drawer for the old book. "SHIPS AND BOATS AND THINGS THAT FLOAT" it said inside the cover. Grandad's writing when he was a kid. He touched the writing sadly.

What was it Grandad's birthday letter had said? It had been tucked in the birthday cards on the bookshelf in his other bedroom. He was glad he'd been the one packing and unpacking his things. He knew exactly where he'd put the birthday cards when he unpacked. He'd shoved them under the stamp album in his desk drawer. Yes, there was the letter still stuck in a birthday card.

"Sometimes the stamps work and sometimes they don't. You can't make them work. The stamp seems to choose you. I'm sure they will help you, just as they helped me."

They hadn't worked for his mother. He remembered

her talking about the fuss Grandad made about the ship stamps and how disappointed he'd been that they didn't affect her. What had he told her? "Perhaps you didn't need them?" or, "Maybe you didn't need them anyway?"

Well Jeremy certainly needed them now. He just wanted out of here for awhile. He had a little trouble finding the magnifying glass, but it was there, too.

Now to pick a stamp. Which stamp would he try this time?

2.

It seemed a very long time ago that he'd discovered the book and stamps in the box from Granny Stark's.

And even though he'd never felt so miserable in his life he wondered if the magic would work. Would he be able to time travel on the ship stamps?

He was almost afraid to turn the pages and smell the musty smell of the old stamps. He could feel his heart beating faster but underneath the excitement there was a tinge of dread. He braced himself for the disappointment that would come if it didn't work.

Which stamp? Something beautiful and free. He needed that. Never mind adventure, he just wanted to get out of here.

There it was. He'd noticed it before. A sailor and a beautiful sailboat. That looked free. And happy. He raised the old magnifying glass to his eye, careful just to look at the fine print on the bottom of the stamp. If it worked, he wanted to know where he was.

"Angus Walters," he read, "Captain." Then captain in French, and then "Bluenose." Right, that famous boat that was on the dime. He'd love to sail on that. He raised his eyes squinting to see the deck itself and slip on board.

It worked! He was on deck, sails belling high over his head, the feel of salt spray in his face. Suddenly he was unbelievably happy. It worked! The stamps and magnifying glass still worked!

He looked down towards his feet. He couldn't see them, of course. Invisible. Just like before.

Until now he hadn't realized how doubtful he'd felt about the stamp working. He couldn't believe how relieved he was as he walked on the deck. It was a rather drunken, wobbly walk. He didn't have his sea legs yet.

There were a lot of people on board. It seemed like a celebration. These sailors at least looked the way he thought sailors should look. Not like the sailors on the *Nonsuch* or the *Northcote.* They wore regular jeans and shirts and there was not a rotten tooth in the lot as far as he could see.

Jeremy moved slowly – the schooner was rocking so much he couldn't have moved quickly if he'd wanted to – toward two men looking anxiously at the instruments. He recognized one as the man on the stamp. Angus Walters – his face older, weather-beaten but still standing steadier than Jeremy could.

He was peering at an antique-looking instrument. Nearby a sailor busy coiling ropes shook his head as Jeremy staggered by.

"Old Capt'n Walters doesn't trust them modern instruments – got his own barometer," he mumbled to himself.

JEREMY CLUNG TO THE RAILING. The *Bluenose* was pitching a lot – more than he liked. He was feeling decidedly queasy now. But he was curious. He wanted to know what was happening.

"Maiden voyage of the *Bluenose II* and we get caught in a hurricane! We were supposed to miss it but it veered and we're right in it." Jeremy overheard a man who nearly collided with him as he made his way slowly along the companionway.

"We can't outrun it," the captain was saying. "We'll heave to and double-reef the foresail...." Walters was staring at the barometer he carried. "The glass is still falling, skipper, the glass is still falling..."

Suddenly the wind stopped. This was what is meant by being in the "eye of the storm," Jeremy realized.

He could see the men working frantically, carrying out the Captain's orders. He realized that he'd better head back to where he'd slipped on board before the wind started again if he didn't want to be blown overboard.

He'd almost made it, drenched and clinging to the railing, when the wind hit again. He was cold and maybe that was lucky. Cold and scared made him forget his seasickness. Almost.

Luckily he knew how to get back home. Just repeat the movement he'd made stepping onto the deck – into the stamp.

It worked! He was back at his desk. Safe.

He could hear his mother in the living room. Vacuuming. He knew by the way things were being slammed into and chairs knocked over that she was not in a good mood. He didn't care. Even mad, it was good to have her there.

3.

So, I guess I "needed" that? He thought wryly. To be scared? Risk my life?

He shuddered, remembering how easily he could have been swept overboard. Nobody would have noticed an invisible boy – a ghost from the future – disappearing in the waves.

Maybe it *had* helped a little. Given him some perspective. Be it ever so screwed up, there's no place like home! He grinned a little.

His mother was vacuuming in the hall now, not as violently as before, or maybe there was nothing to knock over.

Just then she dropped the vacuum, left it running and came in giving him another of the bone-crushing hugs.

"Oh Jer-Bear! What are we going to do?" She was in tears again.

Jeremy hugged her back wondering if his vertebrae would survive.

"It's okay, Mum," he said. Not because he really believed it but because he hoped that would help.

It really wasn't okay at all. It wasn't okay that the person who was being fought over wasn't being told what was going on, and it wasn't okay that nobody bothered to ask him how he felt about the whole thing, and it definitely wasn't okay that until he knew what *was* going on he didn't know how he felt about it.

He'd never even visited Dad for a holiday and now he was supposed to move in?

He wanted to yell. "Would somebody please tell me what's going on?" But he knew that would just upset his mother more. She seemed to be calming down now, patting him on the back and then taking a Kleenex from her pocket to dry her eyes.

"You're right," she said. "We'll manage." She turned and walked back to the hall. "But I don't know how I'm going to pay the lawyer..."

Right, Jeremy thought. There was never enough money. His mother budgeted pretty carefully and she certainly knew a hundred ways to cook hamburger, but every so often, when the car insurance or the house insurance or the taxes came due, she'd be depressed because all the other bills would get behind. Every time she started the car these days she'd pat the dash and say, "Just give me a few more years and don't ask for more than a tune-up, Carla, old girl!"

The vacuum cleaner was switched off now. Jeremy

could hear his mother in her bedroom. He got up. Maybe there was some leftover meatloaf from last night in the fridge and he could make a pickle and meatloaf sandwich. If he put everything away and carefully wiped the counter he might not get yelled at.

"Oh good, Wendy, you're there. I was all ready for the answering machine..." His mother's voice drifted out as he walked by her room.

Jeremy assumed what he thought was the sly look of Super Sleuth. The sandwich would have to wait. He'd listen to the conversation on the other phone. Maybe learn something. Anything was better than what he knew now and worth the risk of getting strung up by the toenails if his mother caught him.

He slithered sleuthlike into the hall by the kitchen and picked up the phone. From here he could see the doorway to his mother's room although if she came through it and caught him on the phone it would be too late. Still, she'd be saying goodbye to Aunt Wendy and that would give him time to hang up. For once he was glad they hadn't been able to afford a carry-around phone.

But when he picked up the phone there wasn't a sound.

"Wendy?" came his mother's voice.

Jeremy was just about to panic and hang up when there was a click and his aunt came back on the line.

"Just switching phones, the battery's dying on the other one."

"Oh," said his mother, "I thought I heard a click..."

Jeremy held his breath. I'm going to have to watch that another time. He'd never listened in on any of the conversations until recently – they were pretty boring usually so why bother? But from now on he knew that he'd be listening a lot. As long as he could get away with it. It was the only way he seemed to have of finding anything out.

"Okay, where were we?" Aunt Wendy was asking.

"Do you think this is because I asked him to increase the support payments? Everything's so much more expensive than it was when we had the divorce agreement...I mean it's not just clothes and all the stuff for soccer and hockey...there's no way I could afford to pay for lessons of any kind. What if he wanted to take piano? I'd have to buy one for starters...."

Jeremy raised his eyes heavenward. Please...*not* piano lessons. Maybe there were advantages to being poor.

"And," his mother went on, her voice rising, "I'd love to get him his own computer, I'm sure it would help him with his homework, but then we'd need internet connections because he'd want to do research...."

Yes! thought Jeremy. Way to go, Mum! Visions of games he could download danced in his head.

"So," said his aunt, "did you mention all this in the letter when you asked for more support?"

His mother was quiet for a little while and Jeremy began to look uneasily towards the bedroom. Was she going to hang up?

"Yes," she sighed. "I was really cheesed off that day, the car insurance was due and Jeremy needed new runners...the kid's feet grow like you wouldn't believe...and, yes, I guess I did more than just ask."

Silence again. Jeremy fidgeted, waiting.

"Uh huh..." said Aunt Wendy, sympathetically.

"I kind of...demanded..."

"And?"

Aunt Wendy was being very patient, Jeremy thought. Why couldn't his mother get on with it?

"And...well...I kind of...I guess I threatened to take him to Court!" His mother finished in a rush.

Jeremy gasped and then hoped it hadn't been too obvious. Maybe his mother would think it was Aunt Wendy? And vice versa?

Aunt Wendy's voice was very calm now. "So...I wonder if Darrin's decided that rather than fork over more money each month, he'll punish you by threatening to take Jeremy? Maybe it's just a threat so you'll back off?"

"And maybe," sighed his mother, "Darrin's new wife can't have children and he's decided that, rather than adopt, he'd rather have his own son to complete his happy home!"

"Ooops!" Aunt Wendy sounded a bit shocked. "I hadn't thought of that...they have been married for nearly five years and there was all that talk of starting a family...."

"Wendy, I just can't stand the thought of losing Jeremy. I love him so much...he's just the best kid...."

"You're right there...he's a fun guy to have around. I wouldn't mind living with him myself."

Wow! thought Jeremy, this is really good. Keep talking!

But just then the doorbell rang. Now what? It was the ding-dong of the front door. What could that be? And what was he going to do? If he hung up now there'd be a click.

Ding-dong. Again. Whoever it was wasn't going away and seemed pretty impatient. They were practically leaning on the doorbell.

"Jeremy!" yelled his mother from her room and nearly deafened him in his phone ear. "Would you please see who it is?"

4.

He was about to panic when he had a stroke of genius. He hung up the phone as quietly as he could and knocked over a kitchen chair almost simultaneously. And then he dashed for the door before it could ring again in case his mother noticed that it wasn't as loud now that the kitchen phone was hung up.

There was a parcel delivery man there. Somehow the man managed to look bored and impatient at the same time. I suppose he practices a lot, Jeremy thought.

"Parcel for Jeremy Thorpe," the man said.

"That's me!"

He thought fast. Not his birthday – Aunt Wendy wasn't on a trip – so who would send him a parcel? It looked like a big one.

The man was holding out a clipboard for him to sign. He tried to read where the parcel came from but he couldn't. The man was in such a hurry. He shoved the big box into Jeremy's arms and was already back at his van.

Jeremy staggered a little from the weight of the box and managed to get into the living room. If he could make it to his bedroom he could set it on the bed or desk and open it there. Otherwise he wasn't sure if he could lift it off the floor. Now he was definitely thankful that they'd moved – he'd never have managed to lug this thing up the stairs.

"Jeremy," his mother was calling from the bedroom, "who was it?"

"Just a delivery man," he yelled back.

He made it into his room. No point in using the desk, it was covered with stuff. The bed wasn't much better but at least the blankets were straight – sort of. He'd made it this morning when he got up just as he was supposed to. But then he'd been lying on it doing the staring-at-the-ceiling thing.

The box really was addressed to him. It was from a computer store.... He couldn't understand it. One minute Mum was worried about money and now she was buying him a computer. Well, something heavy from a computer store. He tried to open the lid of the box. No luck. It was taped down everywhere. He fished in his desk drawer for his jack-knife.

He'd just managed to get the box open and start to take a look when his mother appeared in the doorway.

"What's that?"

He looked up smiling. "I don't know yet." He was struggling to get the styrofoam pads off the top. They sure packed these things well.

"It's whatever you ordered for me, I guess. It had my name on it."

His mother was beside him now. He hadn't known she could move so fast. She pushed him away, closed the box and looked at the label. "Best Buy Computers," she read on the label. "That's here in town! Don't touch anything, I'm going to phone them!"

She was gone, leaving him stunned and really confused. He followed her out to the phone, where she was busy looking through the Yellow Pages and in serious danger of ripping out a few in her hurry.

Best not to say anything. Maybe it wasn't supposed to come until later. Maybe she'd started buying it for Christmas and somebody had made a mistake. Jeremy just stood waiting as she spoke to someone at the store about the parcel. When she hung up there was a look on her face he'd never seen before. Sad and furious all in one.

"It's from your father."

Jeremy was stunned. A real present? He never got a real present. Money for his birthday and money for Christmas – the usual cheque from his dad's office. And his mother usually had to use some for his clothes and then they'd buy a little present. Except last birthday he'd got a skateboard with the money.

"But..." he started to say "he doesn't send presents" but all he said was, "...it's a present!"

"It's a bribe!" His mother mumbled to herself. Then,

to him, "And it has to go back to the store!" She was starting to get angry.

"But..." Jeremy began. He didn't even know what it was. And he didn't even know what this was all about.

His mother had pushed by him and was in his room closing up the box and dragging it to the front door.

By rights this is when I should throw a tantrum, I guess, Jeremy thought, but he was feeling numb again so he just stood there.

He heard the front door slam and then the car door and still he stood there. Maybe I should be running after the car, yelling and crying, he thought.

He remembered once a couple of years ago he'd snooped for his Christmas present. Usually he couldn't find where his mother hid them but this time he'd looked in her jewelry drawer and there it was – the watch he'd been wanting. She'd walked in and caught him just then and taken it from him.

"It's going back to the store!" she said.

And he'd protested. Boy, had he ever protested! Thrown a royal tantrum that time.

"It's not a game of hide and seek," she said. "There's just you and me and we've got to have an honour system. Private property. Private places."

So after he'd picked himself up off the floor, he'd been pretty careful. And she was too. She didn't even empty the pockets of his jeans, that was his job. Pockets were private.

He'd respected privacy until now. What was the

saying? Desperate times call for desperate measures? Now he was listening in on her phone conversations – definitely an invasion of privacy.

The watch had been wrapped and under the tree with his other presents Christmas morning. But thinking about it now helped. A little.

Of course he hadn't actually *seen* the computer. If it had been set up and he'd been using it he'd probably be doing the tantrum thing again. This way it didn't seem real.

Actually the watch was the last tantrum he'd tried. He thought perhaps it meant he was growing up. Maybe it just meant that he was smart enough to figure out that they didn't work with his mother.

How do grown-ups manage to live without throwing tantrums when things are awful? Maybe they just put their kid's new computer in the car and take it back to the store?

The doorbell rang and he walked woodenly to the door.

The same delivery man, definitely not looking pleased this time.

5.

WHAT NOW? JEREMY WONDERED. IF HE'S COME TO GET the parcel back because there was a mistake, he's out of luck. Besides it *was* Jeremy's name on the box.

"Yes?" he said politely.

The delivery man didn't say anything, just shoved the clipboard at him and pointed at the spot to sign. There was his name again. Jeremy signed. He was about to ask what for, when the man snatched the clipboard back and hurried to the truck. That was when Jeremy saw the carton on the front step.

Oh, so this time he doesn't even hand it to me. It isn't *my* fault you didn't notice there were two boxes to deliver, he thought.

It was rather a relief to feel grumpy instead of hurt and confused. He stared at the box on the step. Why not just leave it there and his mother could haul it back to the store when she got back. But it looked like rain, so he bent to pick it up.

This was obviously the monitor and luckily not as heavy as the other box. He set it on the floor just inside the door. His mother could trip over it when she got home for all he cared.

He slammed the door of his room and threw himself on the bed. Yes, he decided, angry was better than sad. At least there was something you could do. Slam doors, kick things and throw things around. He got up again looking for something to kick or throw.

Once, when he was mad, he'd kicked his dresser really hard, forgetting that he didn't have his runners on. His toe had swollen and he couldn't get his runners on for the whole weekend.

He looked at the desk. Lots of stuff to throw, but he'd just have to pick everything up and the stamps would make a big mess. And he didn't want to throw or kick now anyway. He just felt like running away. And he knew how to do it.

There was the *Bluenose*. It worked. Were there other stamps that would work now?

He sat down and started turning the pages of the album. Back to earlier ones, ones Grandad had put in.

There was the *Northcote* stamp and the other river boats. Even some native canoes and a kayak. Maybe later. He wanted some old sailing ship. Something long, long ago.

There was one. 1497 – 1947 it said on the stamp. Wow! 1497 – that was just five years after Columbus sailed the ocean blue! He picked up the magnifying glass, reading the small print under the picture. "Cabot's Matthew" and underneath "Newfoundland."

Cabot was the first to land in what eventually became Canada, he remembered. This would be the earliest ship he'd been on.

He was avoiding looking at the ship itself. This time when he went on board he meant to be ready, braced for the movement of the ship. He took a deep breath and raised the glass.

He had braced himself for being plunged into a storm or rough seas at least, but it wasn't bad at all. And it was sunny.

No problem there. Except he'd landed right by the main mast of the ship and he hadn't noticed a sailor scrambling down the rigging who landed beside him and sent him sprawling.

He wasn't hurt but he lay there getting his breath back which was probably a good thing, for the sailor grabbed a belaying pin and began to flail around until one of his mates came along and demanded to know what happened.

"'Tis the ghost!" The man stared wild-eyed around him. "It touched me! Barty yesterday 'n me today. Maybe 'tis true what the others said..."

His companion broke into a rather mean-looking grin and looked up the rigging the man had just come down.

"You got a tot o' rum tucked away in the mains'el, Doggy?"

That evidently shocked the sailor out of his fear. He

assumed a look of innocence. At least, Jeremy decided, that was what he was attempting, though on that weather-beaten face it could have been anything.

There might have been more to the confrontation, but suddenly the men were distracted. Someone had called out from above them.

"Land!" breathed the second man. "I knew they was shorebirds and we was nearin' land!"

Both men turned to the rail and that gave Jeremy a chance to pull himself to his feet. He followed them at a safe distance. This time as well as looking over his shoulder a lot to make sure no one would walk into him from behind, he was more careful about what was above him just in case.

He was puzzled though. What was this talk about a ghost yesterday? He hadn't been here before. Ever.

Oh well, olden days sailors, he remembered, from his trip on the *Nonsuch* last year, were *very* superstitious.

He strained his eyes to the horizon but could see nothing, though there were flocks of birds now. It was amazing!

Birds of all sizes and shapes, more than he'd ever seen before. In one place they seemed so thick he wondered how they flew without bumping into each other. A mass of dark forms spinning ceaselessly, like when he threw raspberries into milk in the blender and they whirled but never quite disappeared.

And yes, now he could see a dark line of cliffs ahead.

He was going to be here at the moment of discovery!

He looked around at the other men. They weren't staring landward any more but at a strangely dressed man standing on the upper deck.

"Cap'n thinks he's found Cathay for the King?"

The other laughed. "He's just doing his noon reading with that 'thing' of his!"

Jeremy walked carefully forward on the ship and climbed to the foredeck. He wanted to get a closer look at the bronze instrument that glinted in the bright sunshine.

He watched as the weighted line swung back and forth. The plate was marked with degrees, and another man was noting them. But with the ship lurching this way, it can't be very accurate, Jeremy thought. If this is going to tell them where they are it's still not much help.

He turned his attention back to the land ahead. He could see the cliffs more clearly from here.

He watched as the captain directed the man at the tiller. They were turning now. It was obvious there was no place to land here.

"Hard a' starboard," someone yelled.

Jeremy was glad he was up here now for men were moving about hauling on ropes and adjusting sails. He was safely out of the way and could watch the birds.

Funny little clown-like birds were skimming the waves just inches above the turbulent water. How did they do it, he wondered. Then one ran smack into a rising wave and plopped into the water. No, he was up again but somebody else got knocked out of the air.

Jeremy almost laughed out loud, they were so cute and funny. Then he remembered the name – puffins! Funny name too. He remembered they'd been on a bird stamp his mother had collected.

She seemed to think that just because he was interested in the ship stamp book of Grandad's that he'd want her old birds and flowers stamp collection kept up to date so she kept throwing these stamps his way. Now he was glad she had. He decided that even stamps useless for time travel could be useful in other ways.

He was aware of a bell ringing somewhere. Maybe they ring bells to celebrate finding land? Except this seemed rather far away. And it was a distinctly familiar modern sound.

The doorbell was ringing. He'd better get back!

6.

THE DOORBELL WAS STILL RINGING IMPATIENTLY WHEN he got there.

He almost expected to see the delivery man again but it was his mother, her arms full of the computer box.

"I'm sorry, Jer-Bear, I was punishing you and none of this is your fault!"

She was about to walk by him into the living room and with her arms full she couldn't see the other carton. Jeremy stopped her before she banged into it. He took the heavy one from her and nodded at the other.

"That came while you were gone...the guy forgot to deliver it the first time."

"Well," she bent and picked it up, "we might as well see if we can put this together for you."

Okay, Jeremy thought, what do I say? If I hadn't been listening in I wouldn't have a clue as to why she was upset in the first place. And now it looked as if she was just going to ignore the whole business of storming off with the computer. And he was supposed to ignore it too. Well, he wasn't going to. At the risk of upsetting her again, he needed to find out what was going on. But how?

His mother was neatly piling books and things off of his desk. He grabbed the stamp book and magnifying glass and tucked them carefully in the drawer again before she could tidy them out of sight somewhere he'd never find them.

He decided the secret would be to act innocent.

"Funny how Dad would send me something like this, isn't it?" He said casually. "He never sends presents for Christmas or birthdays. Do you think it's a back-to-school present?"

He waited. His mother was still piling things on the bookshelf. Maybe saying that had been a mistake. It might get her back on the "bribe" stuff. He decided that if it did he'd make her explain it this time. Easy enough to do. Innocence again – "But why would he want to bribe me?" would be the obvious response, wouldn't it?

She wasn't answering. Now what? He couldn't ask again.

Finally, the desk was clear. His mother turned and gave him a hug. It wasn't a bone-crusher, just a normal, "it's okay" hug. Then she sighed.

"All right, I should have told you sooner, I guess. How about when we finish setting this thing up, we have a Major Talk. Meanwhile," she handed him the instruction book, "you read and I'll do."

Two hours later, his mother turned to him and shrugged hopelessly. "Who do we know who's a computer whiz?"

Tough question. He knew all about computers himself – if they were set up and sitting in the school library.

"I guess my friend Charlie's dad," Jeremy said. "At least he's got one and uses it all the time."

"So phone Charlie and see when we can get some help."

Jeremy looked at her. Was she postponing the Major Talk? While he wasn't exactly looking forward to it, it would be the first time a Major Talk hadn't meant he was in serious trouble.

"Charlie's on holidays. Remember?" He couldn't believe she hadn't noticed how hard it had been for him the past couple of weeks with his best – he had to admit his only – friend out of town. "He won't be back until next week just before school starts."

Then the phone rang, but his mother was already out the door. He didn't dare try to listen to this one.

He decided to wander out into the hall – maybe he could at least figure out who was calling.

Too late. She was hanging up when he got there.

She looked up and said, "I've got a surprise for you!"

7.

THERE WAS A RATHER SMUG, MYSTERIOUS LOOK ON HIS mother's face, a kind of "I'll give you three guesses look". Jeremy didn't feel like guessing games right now. A surprise could be anything. More computer stuff even. No, he didn't think so. His mother looked too pleased.

"So what is it?" he demanded.

She just smiled and said, "I'll be back in about an hour. Then you'll see!" as she rushed to the front door. "A shame we couldn't get that computer working – you'd have something to do while you're waiting." At that the door slammed behind her.

Don't worry, Jeremy thought, I've got plenty to do. An hour was great! Before he did anything though he wanted to know a little more about Cabot.

He waited until he heard his mother's car pull away then sprinted into her room to the shelf where she kept the encyclopedia. The Canadian one would be best, and besides it was newest.

Not much on "Cabot" – a lot more on "Cable Television".

> Cabot, John (Giovanni Caboto) b. about 1450 in Genoa. In 1461 he went to live in Venice.... Independently of Columbus, Cabot seems to have conceived the idea of reaching Asia by sailing westward across the Atlantic. About 1484 he moved with his family to London. In 1496 Henry VII granted him letters patent authorizing him "to seek out, discover and find" any hitherto unknown lands.
>
> Cabot sailed from Bristol on May 2, 1497, in a small ship, the *Matthew.* Fifty-two days later on June 24, 1497, he made a landing on the North American coast – either in Newfoundland, southern Labrador or Cape Breton Island.

Wow! Maybe he could be there when Cabot made his famous landfall to put up the king's flag. If he could be there he could solve the mystery of where he really landed and figure out what was going on aboard the *Matthew* too!

Back in his room he dug the stamp book and magnifying glass out of the drawer. The computer was in the way. It didn't leave enough room on the desk to sit the way he had before. He wondered if that would affect the way it worked.

He'd soon find out, he decided, as he piled up the pillows on his bed. If he pulled up the quilt, and he was still on board the ship when his mother got back it would just look as though he was asleep. If the stamp worked again, that is.

He tried to ignore the knot of "maybe-it-won't-work-this-time fear" that always seemed to sit like a heavy lump in his stomach and settled himself, the book in his lap, the magnifying glass in his hand as he focussed on the old green stamp.

This time he was back in exactly the same place, standing right by the main mast of the old ship.

They were now sailing parallel to the cliffs along the coast. He wondered how far they had sailed while he was gone.

There was a bay ahead. Perhaps they were going to anchor here? Jeremy hoped they would go ashore. It would be wonderful to be there, setting foot on the new land with Cabot.

He began to wander carefully around the ship. It looked as if this was an anchorage all right.

He stopped to watch as some men were lowering weighted wooden buckets over the side of the ship. Funny kind of anchor? But no, after a little while the buckets were pulled up and dumped, and dozens of fish were flopping about on the deck. Not for long!

The men were happily scooping them up and disappearing below deck. Jeremy could guess what was happening. Fresh fish chowder for supper. A change from sea rations – no wonder they were smiling.

Now his attention was caught by two rowboats being lowered over the side of the ship. He was caught in a dilemma.

He wanted so much to go ashore. And more than that he wanted to see what Cabot saw.

But how to get on one of the boats without being stepped on going down the rope ladder, or bumped into in the boat? He didn't want anyone panicking about ghosts again. He'd seen the reaction last time.

All the same he slipped closer to the ladder that dangled over the side of the ship. The first men had already gone down into the boat, grabbing the oars and steadying it near the ship. Now, they were standing back waiting for Cabot to go.

Jeremy seized his chance and slipped over the rail. If Cabot stepped on his fingers, at least he'd be the only person in Canada alive today who'd had that happen to him!

Trouble was because there was supposed to be nobody on the ladder, the sailors below weren't bothering to hold it and it was swinging against the side of the ship. Jeremy tried to shift himself so that he wasn't bashed up too much. Only by holding on for dear life with one hand and keeping one arm out to keep the ship away could he manage. And then, of course, he couldn't let go to go down the next step.

The problem was solved as the captain came over the rail and began his descent. A sailor below grabbed the end of the swinging ladder and held it steady. Now Jeremy's only problem would be to avoid bumping the man when he tried to jump onto the boat.

He tried not to think about it – aimed for a pile of rope in the bottom of the boat and jumped.

Lucky for him, there was enough noise from the sea and the shouts of the men that no one noticed the thud of his fall. And the boat was rocking anyway. And everyone was focussed on watching the captain's descent.

So he was safe in the longboat. Safe – if you didn't consider that he'd really fallen hard and hurt his knee, though being invisible he couldn't see how much damage he'd really done. He could certainly "feel" it though and it wasn't good. He felt for blood but who could tell? There was enough water in the boat that he didn't know whether the wet feeling was blood or water.

He crouched there in the bottom of the boat feeling sorry for himself and hoping no one would step on him. The boat obviously had everyone who was going along already aboard. And the men began to row ashore while the other boat was still loading.

Jeremy counted. There were ten on board counting Cabot and himself. He looked back at the other boat. Only six coming in that one. That left only two or three men still on the ship. At least he hadn't counted any more.

With all the oarsmen it didn't take them long to get to shore.

Jeremy waited until most of the men got out before he

slipped into the water to wade ashore. Evidently two of the men were going to stay in the boat while the others went ashore.

Of course, he thought, they didn't know what they'd meet and might have to leave in a hurry. It was only as he struggled to the beach that he noticed that some of the men were carrying weapons. Crossbows, he guessed. He'd seen pictures. They looked awfully awkward to handle.

He limped up onto the beach. Maybe the cold water had numbed the pain in his knee a bit. He could walk quite well. And it was good to be on land again.

Then he realized what he'd done. Land! He was on land! Not on the *Matthew* – not on the stamp of the *Matthew*.

How could he have been so dumb?

If anything happened and he had to get home, he didn't have a hope.

8.

ALL THE EXCITEMENT HE SHOULD HAVE FELT ABOUT being part of this historic moment was deadened by the sick feeling he had.

His mother would come home to a sleeping boy – a boy who'd never wake up unless he could figure out a way to get back on the ship.

He looked back toward the longboats. The second one had unloaded and the men were coming ashore but they'd left one behind in that boat too. No chance of sneaking back to the boat, knocking the sailor overboard and hijacking it. Besides could one kid row such a heavy boat all the way to the ship? The guys in the other boat could easily catch him. They wouldn't know there was someone in it, of course, just think it was drifting away.

Forget it. Might as well keep an eye on Cabot and look around. That's why he'd done this dumb thing in the first place. He'd just have to hope nothing happened so that he couldn't make it back on board the *Matthew*.

The men with crossbows had moved ahead up the beach towards higher ground. Everyone moved cautiously, scanning the thick stand of tall spruce trees that edged the shoreline.

At a point of higher ground, Cabot had stopped and the men with him were erecting not one, but two flags.

One was very plain. A cross, red on a white background. The other was much more impressive. It was red and gold and seemed to be a lion standing with his foot on a book.

Too bad guys, Jeremy thought, noticing the wooden flag staffs. If you'd used a pole made of metal maybe somebody could have found them someday and identified the spot.

That gave him an idea. He searched his pockets. Perhaps he could bury something and then find this place again and prove that this was the place Cabot had landed.

All he had was a quarter. A 1999 quarter. He could bury that! For a moment he felt excitement and then he realized that wouldn't prove a thing. He might come back next year or the year after and even if – and it was pretty shaky that he'd even recognize the place – what would finding a 1999 quarter in 2003 or any time after that, prove?

He put the quarter back in his pocket. Now if Cabot or somebody were to drop a coin, *that* would be useful. He watched the men carefully but none of them looked as if they would even *have* money let alone drop any.

"Capt'n!" Some of the men further into the clearing in the woods were calling.

The flag-raising was finished. Cabot had said something about claiming the land, at least that was what Jeremy figured it was – he couldn't understand a word. He supposed Cabot was speaking his native Italian.

He followed as the men excitedly pointed to the remains of a campfire with a few things lying about. There seemed to be a pot made of birch bark and some other bits of wood. But what looked the most interesting to Jeremy was a carved red stick about half a metre long.

The men were interested too. They were passing it around to examine it. Jeremy risked bumping into someone trying to get close enough to look at it. He could see that it was hand-made and the red colouring had been applied somehow.

"Brazil?" One of the men said. They seemed to agree on that, though Jeremy could have told them that whether this was Labrador or Newfoundland or Cape Breton Island, it didn't matter – they were a long way from Brazil. But no, they were pointing to the colour of the stick. The red of it.

Now he could have helped them on that. Last year, in Mrs. Das's Social Studies class they'd been studying the Beothuks, that lost tribe of Newfoundland, and she'd read them a book called *Blood Red Ochre.* He'd really liked that part of the course.

These people, the Beothuks, used red ochre to colour

everything, even their faces, and that was why the early explorers had called the inhabitants of North America "Red Indians". So this was probably what was on the stick. Red ochre. Which meant the landing had been in Newfoundland.

He *really* wanted to get a good look at the stick now. But he couldn't, the men were moving away and one had rolled the stick in a bundle of cloth and tucked it inside his tunic. All Jeremy had seen was that the top of the stick was carved in a series of triangles, one fitting into the other. If there was any detail on the flat surfaces he'd missed it.

Beyond this campground the men had found a trail into the forest, but here the trees were very close together and any number of people could have been hiding – waiting and watching.

The crew were obviously nervous about attack. They would move only far enough up the trail that a companion could cover them with the crossbow. Just like cops on a chase in a TV show.

Jeremy looked anxiously at the sky. The sun had dropped quite a bit though it was still a long way from setting.

What had the encyclopedia said? June 24th, 1497? So it was near the longest day of the year. And in Edmonton at that time of year the sun didn't set until after ten o'clock at night.

He shut his eyes and tried to visualize the map of

Canada Mrs. Das had hanging on the wall of her classroom. He was pretty sure that Newfoundland was about the same latitude as Edmonton, maybe even a little further North.

He wondered what time it was. He was wearing his watch but a fat lot of good it did him. He couldn't see his wrist or his arm.

Now he noticed that Cabot's men were returning to the boats.

He managed a kind of limping run down to the shore and plunged into the water. He had to get to the longboat ahead of the men. They had longer legs and could wade better than he could. Some of them were already nearly at the boat.

Probably just as well that everyone was moving so noisily. He'd wondered too late what kind of splashing and displacement of water he was making. Luckily no one noticed anything unusual. And, to his relief he was able to scramble onto one side of the boat as men were clambering over the other side so nobody noticed it rocking strangely. It was rocking a lot anyway.

He'd have heaved a sigh of relief, but he still had to worry about getting up that ladder.

Now the men were rowing very fast, looking back over their shoulders. At what? They seemed afraid that the people would come back to their camp or start shooting at the boats. There was no one to use the crossbows now since everyone except himself and Cabot were busy with the oars.

Luckily the boat came alongside the ship on Jeremy's side. The ladder dangled just in reach. If he could start up it first he'd be okay.

The rope was wet and slippery but he managed to get a grip and make a kind of a jump for it. Trying not to think about his sore leg he pulled himself up to the first rung, then the second and just kept scrambling. Someone had grabbed the bottom and was getting ready to get on but by that time Jeremy was nearly to the top, looking down and moving as quickly as his sore leg would let him.

He realized the man coming up next was Cabot and he was taking his time. Jeremy slowed down too. Good thing! He'd almost climbed right into the face of the sailor at the railing who was leaning over the rail looking down at the men in the boats below.

Oh-oh! thought Jeremy miserably. If this guy doesn't get out of the way before Cabot gets to my feet, I won't have anywhere to go! He stared down at the cold water frothing below. It seemed a very long way down.

9.

JEREMY HELD HIS BREATH. THE SAILOR JUST ABOVE HIM wasn't moving and Cabot was climbing steadily up the rope ladder. It was going to be close.

Could he reach the railing without bumping into the man and work his way hand over hand along it? He didn't like the idea of dangling all that way above any more than he liked the idea of falling down into the water below.

Then he realized the man above him was none other than the sailor who'd bumped into him by the mast. Doggy? The guy who'd been so upset because of ghosts? That gave him idea. If it worked it would get the man out of the way – and if it didn't he wouldn't be any worse off than he was before.

Unless Doggy could find a weapon. But that thought crossed his mind too late. He'd already reached out his hand and growled in his best Long John Silver voice, "Be gone wit' ye Doggy!"

He knew his hand was nearly frozen from the icy

water and it only touched Doggy's for a moment but it had the effect he wanted.

The man sprang back with a cry and Jeremy scrambled quickly over the railing and made his escape. His last view of the men on board the *Matthew* was of Doggy clutching his hand and mumbling, "The ghost! 'E touched me with 'is icy hand!"

JEREMY WAS THANKFUL that he'd covered himself in bed so that he'd look asleep. He could hear voices in the kitchen. His mother and Aunt Wendy! Right! So that had been the surprise. I wonder what she brought me!

He started to climb out of bed wondering how long they'd been here. He could smell the makings of supper. Great! He was starving.

And freezing. He'd sneak into the bathroom and soak his hands in hot water. He didn't want Aunt Wendy to feel the "ghostly hand" when he gave her a hello hug.

He could hear his mother's voice clearly as he came out of the bedroom.

"I guess my first step is going to be to see a lawyer." She sounded choked up. "One of my friends at work says she knows of one who works on custody litigation."

"You sure it's not just a bluff?" Aunt Wendy sounded as though she had her mouth full. She was always tasting things in the kitchen. The thought made Jeremy's stomach rumble so loudly he was sure they'd hear him.

"You mean because I asked for more support?" His mother was talking with her mouth full too – it just wasn't fair! "Even if he is...I really do need the extra money...I just can't stay caught up with the bills. I'm going to have to fight!"

Jeremy tucked his hands under his sweatshirt, shuddering as they touched his bare skin. He couldn't go in the bathroom now. He was finding out things. Maybe he could get his hands warm enough this way.

"You know I've got some RRSP's...I could lend you a little money...."

"No, I'll manage somehow!" There was that final note in his mother's voice Jeremy recognized only too well. "Do you think this sauce needs more spices – a little more oregano?"

"Mmmm...no, Sandy, it's perfect as always!"

Aunt Wendy was laughing. Obviously the serious talk was over and his hands weren't too bad. He started down the hall and then realized that he should be running and excited and ready for greetings.

"Aunt Wendy!" He said running the last few steps. "You were the surprise!"

Then it was laughing and hugs and Jeremy couldn't wait to sit down to supper – the smell of his mother's spaghetti sauce was overwhelming. Actually he *did* manage to wait while Aunt Wendy rummaged in her suitcase for the latest shirt. It was a super skateboarder sweatshirt. Nice and loose and he was tempted to go put it on right away. It looked cosy and he was still feeling chilly but he knew if he did he'd probably get tomato sauce all over it. And besides he wanted to eat *now!*

"So, what's the plan for after supper, kiddo?"

He'd long ago decided that he much preferred Aunt Wendy's pet name for him – "kiddo" – to his mother's "Jer-Bear". He guessed they'd both been calling him those names since he was little, but "Jer-Bear" made him remember the crib full of bears he used to sleep in and *that* was definitely baby-land. Even after his mother had finally moved him into a regular bed, the crib full of bears stayed in his room almost until he'd started school.

He'd always thought it was amazing how different the two sisters were. They didn't even look like sisters. Aunt Wendy had honey-blond hair, always smooth and shiny like a model or a movie star. Mum's hair was plain brown – "mouse brown" she called it – worn in a short, "practical, no-fuss" cut. And even though his mother was the elder by two years she looked much older than Aunt Wendy. Maybe it was the smiles that did it. Mum didn't smile much, especially these days.

He knew Aunt Wendy was waiting for an answer but his mouth was full – this was great spaghetti. His mother had really been generous with the hamburger in the sauce for a change.

"Ummm," he said and waved to his room.

His mother laughed. "I think he's trying to tell you we were attempting to put together the computer in his room...the one I told you about."

Jeremy caught his mother giving Aunt Wendy "a look", the kind grown-ups used when they wanted to refer to things that kids weren't supposed to know about. It was the kind of look kids learned to figure out pretty early on.

And of course they'd have had the drive back from the airport to discuss things like "the bribe".

There was no more discussion that night. There was ice cream and pie – his mother had stopped at the store on the way home. This really was a celebration.

Lucky for him Aunt Wendy's favourite pie was pecan just like his. Actually he had to admit that almost *any* pie was his favourite but they hardly ever had pie any more.

"So you're having trouble getting the computer hooked up?" Aunt Wendy was wiping her lips and folding her napkin. "We'll just leave the dishes to your mother and see what we can do. Computers are my business."

That was right! Jeremy had forgotten she used to work in a computer store selling them before she got the job as a programmer.

And it didn't take her a minute to figure out what was wrong. She checked all the cords and wiggled everything and then laughed and got down under the desk.

"Your mother plugged everything into the surge bar but she neglected to plug that in! Voila! You press that button now, kiddo!"

And there it was... working. At last! His own computer. Now, he *was* excited. This was great! He was sure he was about the only kid in his class who didn't have a computer at home.

"Hmmm, that's nice," said Aunt Wendy, "it's even got a *World Book* encyclopedia installed. I know you'd much rather have that than a bunch of games!"

"Yeah, right!" He was laughing. Then he got an idea. He'd show her. He clicked on the icon and searched for Cabot.

> In May, 1497, Cabot sailed west from Bristol in a small ship, the *Matthew*, with a crew 18 sailors. The crew sighted land on June 24 and went ashore. No one knows exactly where Cabot landed. Most historians say he may have landed somewhere between what are now Newfoundland and Nova Scotia.

It was pretty much the same stuff he knew, but it did say that Cabot had a crew of eighteen just as he'd figured. That made him feel good. It didn't mention the second flag though and he wondered about that.

10.

JEREMY LAY IN BED THAT NIGHT. THE COMPUTER WAS great even though he didn't have an Internet connection yet. Still, it wasn't like being on board ships and learning about things by being there.

His mother and aunt had stayed up until just a few minutes ago. He'd kept his door open so he could listen to what they were talking about. He wasn't any wiser about the so-called lawsuit. All his mother had talked about was money and how desperately they needed it. He knew she didn't make much working in the office at Majestic Moving & Storage. Even without legal fees, it sounded as if things were much worse than he'd realized. Maybe they should have found a house with a smaller mortgage sooner.

He sighed. Was there anything he could do to help? He already had a flyer route so that he wouldn't need an allowance, but he didn't think that a few dollars a week made that much difference. Not the way his mother was talking. She needed several thousand dollars just to get things back on an even keel, she'd said.

"Back on keel," obviously that was a saying that must have started at sea. He'd been surprised to discover how many everyday things came from sailing days. "Learning the ropes," for example. The sailors he'd watched certainly "knew the ropes" and it looked very complicated to know which ropes were used for which sails.

He lay there, unable to sleep. He might as well take another trip. Maybe he could find out more about the "ghost" business. His mother and Aunt Wendy were probably asleep by now.

Now that he knew that he could use the stamps when he was lying on his bed it would just look as if he'd fallen asleep. He tiptoed over and quietly closed his door so he could turn on his bedside light. He'd have left the light turned out, but that way he couldn't look into the stamp and onto the deck of the *Matthew*.

This time the ocean was not as smooth as Jeremy would have liked. Still, he was managing quite well as he carefully moved across the deck.

It was night here too, only two men that he could see, and they were on the foredeck safely out of the way.

He looked up. At least it was a clear night. Had he ever seen so many stars? He didn't think so. It couldn't be that they had disappeared in modern times. It must be because there were no city lights around to diminish them. Out here on the ocean it was truly dark and even if there was land nearby who would be there? No towns with lighted streets and buildings anyway. It was beautiful. He felt as if he could almost reach out and scoop his hand through the Milky Way or grab the handle of the Big Dipper.

He walked towards the rail, easing into the movement of the boat, still looking up at the brilliant sky.

Then just as he reached it he hit something – something or someone who wasn't there!

He even heard the soft intake of breath, a sort of "oof" sound coming from nowhere. He'd made the same sort of sound himself, but not quite, and anyway he was sure the sound hadn't come from his own mouth.

He moved again – and bumped again. "What the?" he mumbled under his breath. He was sure his voice would be muffled by the waves. Anyway the sailors on the foredeck were much too far away to hear him.

This time there wasn't a sound. Was something still there?

He reached out and grabbed a piece of cloth. It felt like a shirt or something. With his other hand he patted along the body until he found an arm.

The other person gave him a shove. "Cut that out!" it said.

Jeremy stumbled on the moving deck and made a dive to grab the rail and catch his balance. This time he didn't bump anyone.

"Who are you?" he mumbled but there was no answer.

Jeremy flailed his arm around, even moved away from the rail, searching. Whoever – whatever it was, was gone.

Maybe Doggy and Bart, the old time sailors, were right. Maybe ships could be haunted.

But it hadn't been a ghostly voice, although he had to admit he'd never heard one. It had been an ordinary, everyday voice a lot like his own. In fact, from the feel of the arm, height and everything it was probably somebody about his own age.

That was probably a good thing, he decided, since he'd have been in big trouble if he'd been poking and grabbing somebody big and mean.

11.

BACK IN HIS ROOM, HE LAY THERE STILL TENSE, STILL worried by what had happened. His mind was racing with possibilities. It didn't take him long to decide that, despite the superstitious sailor talk, this was *not* a ghost. After all, they thought *he* was a ghost.

A proper ghost would not say, "Cut that out!" in a normal boy's voice. And besides ghosts were not supposed to be solid things you bumped into.

According to all the horror shows he'd seen and Halloween stories he'd read, ghosts were supposed to appear, look transparent, and if you touched them your hand went right through – like punching cobwebs or mist.

Not a ghost. At least, Jeremy decided, not a ghost any more than he was.

And, of course, that was it! The sailors thought he was a ghost but he wasn't. He was a time traveller.

So what if that's who the other guy was? – a time traveller like him!

Suddenly, he felt very tired. He'd think about all of this in the morning.

AUNT WENDY WAITED FOR HIM to get up before she started making the waffles. His mother had long since left for work.

"Wow, kiddo, you were really dead to the world when I looked in after your ma left." Aunt Wendy was laughing as she plopped the hot, crisp waffles onto his plate. "I thought you'd already turned off that computer before I went to bed. Turned it back on did you? Pretty sneaky! No wonder you're tired out."

Jeremy concentrated on smearing butter all over the waffle. He let it melt nicely into all the little holes before he reached for the syrup. He didn't say anything, just grinned up at his aunt. Let her think that. She obviously wasn't upset about it.

"Ummmm," he said with his first mouthful. That could be interpreted as a "yes" or a "these waffles are great!"

"Eat up, kiddo, there's more where that came from!" She popped another batch hot from the waffle iron onto a plate on the table. "Besides, you're going to need your strength.... You and I are going shopping this morning!"

He looked up, surprised.

"Yeah, pardner," she said sitting down across from him with her coffee. "We're going to ride off to the mall and get you some back-to-school clothes and supplies. I thought we could surprise your ma."

He hated the thought of shopping, even with Aunt Wendy, but it was nice of her. And it would be one less thing his mother had to worry about buying. So he nodded, even though he'd much rather be home alone with the stamps trying to see if he could meet up with that "ghost" again.

They returned home loaded with bags of shirts and jeans and more scribblers than he figured he'd need in the next two years of school, not to mention flow pens and paints and even a calculator which he didn't think he'd get to use at school but it would sure come in handy for math homework.

Aunt Wendy threw herself down on the couch in the living room where she'd slept the night before.

"I don't know about you, kiddo, but I'm pooped. Want anything to eat?"

Normally Jeremy's answer to that would have been a resounding, "Yes!" but they'd stopped for a pizza on the way home and he was still full.

"No," he said dumping the bags on the easy chair and floor where his mother could check everything out. She'd do that anyway, might as well make it easy for her. "I'll just go to my room for a bit."

Aunt Wendy grinned. "Oh-oh! I've kept you from the computer all this time, haven't I. Go to it, kiddo!"

Jeremy was almost to his room when she called after him.

"Just a minute, Jeremy!"

That really stopped him in his tracks. She never called him Jeremy. He turned back, puzzled.

"Ummmm, kiddo..."

It was funny to see Aunt Wendy fumbling for words but he couldn't think of anything to say to help.

"...I know the computer is a big deal and it's really great for you to have one...."

There was the hesitation again. What should he say? "Yeah, it's great," he said but not too enthusiastically because she seemed to want that.

"But don't...ummm...don't let it seem too much that way when your ma's around? I mean it was really good last night when she saw you still seemed to be interested in those old stamps."

Now he understood. It was the bribe thing again. He'd noticed with other kids there was a sort of rivalry between parents who were divorced. The one the kid lived with would be upset, sort of jealous, if the other parent bought or did something and the kid was happy about it. He'd never experienced it before. It had always been just Mum and him. No rivalry. Until now. Now, what Aunt Wendy was trying to say was, "Be cool."

"Right," he said and turned back to his room.

It wasn't the computer he wanted to get to right now anyway. It was the "old stamps". One old stamp in particular – the *Matthew*.

12.

THIS TIME HE NOT ONLY WORRIED ABOUT BEING BUMPED into by one of the sailors, he worried about being bumped into by the "other ghost".

Or was he? Actually, he wanted to meet this other person. He wanted to grab him and hold on and just find out where he came from and how he'd learned the trick of time-travelling.

So many questions flooded Jeremy's mind. Was the other kid travelling on a *Matthew* stamp too? How had he learned how to do it? Stuff like that. Of course he wanted to know how old he was and where he was from and those things as well.

But maybe he wasn't going to learn anything today. There seemed to be a bit of trouble on board the ship.

Two men were standing above them on the foredeck arguing with Cabot.

Other men stood back and were watching. Jeremy

couldn't really read their looks but he doubted that they were on Cabot's side.

A couple of sailors nearby were only pretending to coil the lines out of the way. Jeremy actually saw one give the neatly coiled ropes a kick so he could start over again.

He was close enough to hear these two.

"Skipper's wrong wit' that astrolabe of 'is. That's wot I sez an' that's what the first mate's sayin' too!"

"Aye. There's not a man jack on board who doesn't think it!" mumbled his companion. "'E's got us headed 'way too far North! Mate sez we'll be landin' in the Shetlands if we follow 'is directions!"

Jeremy sidled around the men. It looked as if the coast was clear to run up the stairs to the deck where the men were gathered around the tiller arguing.

Halfway there though, it happened again. Something solid where nothing should be. It took him by surprise but he recovered quickly and grabbed. And caught hold of somebody's shirt. Flannel it felt like. He was getting ready to see if he could find an arm to hold onto when he realized that this time the person wasn't going to wriggle away.

This time he'd been grabbed right back. The other person was hanging on to him!

Neither of them said anything but the other boy was stronger and he was pushing Jeremy back beyond the sailors and their coils of rope to the aft part of the deck where there was no one.

Once they were there the other boy stopped pushing and just hung on to him. Jeremy did the same.

"Okay!" hissed the boy. "Who are you and what are you doing here?

"I...I could ask you the same thing!" He stammered.

"Yeah, I guess so!" The boy's whisper changed. Softer, not as threatening. "Okay, we'll take turns. You aren't from this time are you?"

Easy question, thought Jeremy. "No. It's past the five hundredth anniversary of Cabot's voyage. What year are you from?"

"1947."

"Oh wow! That's the year the *Matthew* stamp came out!" Jeremy forgot himself and talked out loud, his voice came out sort of shrill.

"So you are using the stamp too? That's incredible!"

Jeremy could feel the other boy let go his arm, grabbing his hand and shaking it.

"How do you do?" he said formally.

"Hi!" said Jeremy shaking back. "I'm Jeremy and you are?"

"Harv..." But he was cut off by the sound of a gruff voice.

"'Oo's back 'ere. I 'ear voices, Bart!"

Two angry shapes appeared. Doggy and another man Jeremy assumed was Bart. The men were looking fiercely around.

"Someone's playin' a trick on us...let's get 'em!

The two hulking men were blocking the way and moving about so that they'd be hard to dodge.

"Every man for himself!" whispered Jeremy's companion. "I'll go to the port side!"

It took Jeremy a moment to remember which was port and which was starboard and then he had to figure out whether the left side was facing front or back so he'd know where port was as he stood. In the time he was standing there Doggy made a grab into thin air and gave him a whack on the side of the head.

"Got 'im!" yelled Doggy. Now several other sailors were running aft and Bart had scooped up a bucket of something.

But Jeremy had by now figured which way it was safe to duck and duck he did, his head ringing as he scrambled away.

"Throw the flour!" Doggy called, "'ee's getting away!"

Jeremy turned in time to see a shower of white descending where he had been only moments before. So Doggy had been planning a ghost trap. It would have worked too.

As he scurried to the place he always came aboard he could hear the laughter and his last sight was of a flour-covered Doggy standing cursing Bart's bad aim.

"So you're the ghost ye've been goin' on about, Doggy!" hooted one of the sailors. "Cook'll make hard tack of you for wastin' 'is flour."

He lay in bed – grateful to be back safely. With a

headache that would have made him go to bed if he hadn't already been there. He just hoped he wouldn't have a bump to explain away.

Still, the trip had been successful, he consoled himself. He'd actually met the other "ghost" and he seemed like a nice kid.

He wished they could have made arrangements to meet again though. It was pretty "iffy" just hoping to run into each other.

Jeremy smiled. "Run into" was the operative word all right. Next time they'd have to arrange a specific spot on the ship to meet.

It would even be a good idea to have a special place for each to stand.

But they had accomplished quite a bit, he thought as he closed the stamp book and went to put it on the desk. He'd better get a cold washcloth and put it on his head to keep it from swelling up like a goose egg.

Yes, they were both using the stamp. And the other kid was named Harv. Jeremy looked down at the stamp book. "Harvey Stark" it said.

Now Jeremy felt a chill as if he'd really walked into a ghost.

Harv...Harvey...the kid he'd bumped into was Grandad!

13.

Why was he so shocked? He should have known that Grandad had time-travelled on the stamps. He did know.

That's what all that funny double-talk in the letter had been about. The part about the stamps "working for you" and "not working for your mother". Of course he'd known.

But this was different. It's one thing to know something and quite another when it's actually happening to you. What was it called? The difference between theory and practice or something. He wasn't sure. It didn't matter.

What mattered was that he'd actually met his own grandfather as a kid. So why was that any different than meeting men on sailing ships? Those men had been dead for hundreds of years and he hadn't had any spine-tingling feelings about that.

But this made him feel as if he'd actually met and

touched a ghost. His heart was pounding. He bet if he took his own pulse it would be racing. He stumbled back to bed and lay down.

What had he been doing? On the way to the bathroom to put a cold cloth on his lumpy head. At least it wasn't aching now. The shock of realization had knocked his headache clean off the map.

He made it to the bathroom just as his mother came in the door. Now what? She'd want him to "model" the new clothes. No way! But he would have to go out into the living room and look enthusiastic.

He held the cold washcloth against his head for a minute. Looking in the mirror he was grateful that he didn't seem to have any signs of swelling on his head yet. There was a red spot but maybe they wouldn't notice.

"Jeremy!" His mother was calling. "Come and model these clothes for me!"

He knew it. Might as well get it over with. He went out into the living room, took a deep breath and said, "Great clothes, huh Mum?" And quickly, before there could be any more mention of modelling, "And they fit great...I tried everything on at the store." He held one of the sweatshirts up against himself to show her.

"Oh, Wendy, you are a lifesaver. I've been dreading this." His mother was looking pleased but a little misty-eyed. "You shouldn't have, really, so much money...."

Luckily Aunt Wendy interrupted before things got too bad. "Hey, it was a pleasure getting stuff for the guy.

He's quite cooperative...if you offer him a big enough pizza bribe!"

When finally all the clothes were folded and put away he settled down at the computer with Aunt Wendy to demonstrate all the stuff he'd figured out. It didn't take long.

"We'll have to see about getting you connected to the Internet for Christmas," she said, "Then you can use your Netscape and do research on excite.com or some of the other places. In the meantime, having the *World Book* is going to be a big help with your homework."

Jeremy had his eye on another icon. He couldn't wait to try the Star Wars Jedi Knight game. Charlie had it and they'd played a bit. He knew it wasn't the latest hot game but it was still fun.

"Okay if I try this? I've played it before."

Aunt Wendy laughed. "I get the hint, kiddo, time I went and visited with my big sister anyway." She got up to go.

Then she saw the stamp book lying on the desk. He'd forgotten to put it away, he'd been so excited.

"Oh yes, Dad's old stamp book. Your mother got into them too but not the way he seemed to want." Her voice was thoughtful. "I didn't even try. I figured if Sandy disappointed him, I didn't stand a chance. He used to tease me that I had the attention span of a butterfly!"

She carefully turned the pages, "Some of these stamps are pretty old, aren't they?"

Her voice sounded strange. Jeremy looked up, but she'd closed the book and put it back without saying anything more. She had a funny look on her face as she left the room. He wondered about that. But not for long. Getting blasters and light sabres and blowing up a few aliens demanded all his attention.

He played until everyone went to bed and his mother stuck her head in the door.

"That's it! Into bed! You can read for fifteen minutes and then lights out.

He didn't even argue. "Right away, Mum!"

Of course he knew she wouldn't believe him. Sure enough, a few minutes later she opened his door and looked in. He almost laughed at the shocked look on her face. He was already in bed, and, knees up, the stamp book propped against them, she couldn't tell what book he was reading.

"Know something?" she said, as she blew him a kiss. "You're a great guy and I love you."

He reached up and caught the kiss just like he used to when he was little. That made his mother smile even more. She would go to bed happy and she wouldn't be checking on him again.

He lay there not quite ready to take another trip on the *Matthew*. He hoped he'd meet the other boy. Grandad! Wow, how would he think about the "other ghost" now. And what would he say?

"Hi! I'm really your grandson Jeremy from the future.

You're dead now, of course and..." What could he say?

Maybe it would be better not to say anything at all right now.

How would he feel if it was the other way around? What if Harv said that to him? He'd feel downright stupid. Pretty uncomfortable. And awkward. And what to answer? Deepen your voice and say, like adults always did, "Hello, son! How's school?"

Nope. It would be best not to say anything. He didn't want to scare the boy Grandad away by making things awkward for him. They'd have a lot to talk about. He was really looking forward to having a friend to talk to. He missed Charlie. And even he wasn't somebody to talk to about the time-travelling on the stamps. What if Charlie told somebody? The kids at school would think he was nuts. And he'd be teased even more than he was now.

He picked up the magnifying glass and stared into it at the deck of the *Matthew*.

Before he knew it he was flat on his back.

The ship was pitching and the deck was slippery. The sea was washing across it and he was being swept along – sluiced like a bug down a rain spout towards the railing.

14.

THE ICY WATER TOOK HIS BREATH AWAY AND THEN HE began to scramble wildly trying to flatten himself out enough to stop being swept overboard. It was useless, hopeless, there was too much water washing on deck and the ship was tilted so that there was nowhere for him to go but overboard. He would slide right under the railing and that would be the end of him.

The water was splashing in his eyes. His only hope was that he could reach up and grab a rail or post just before he went overboard. But even if he did, could he hold on?

He kept on moving, scrambling desperately. And then he managed to grab one of the ropes that had come uncoiled and washed about the deck. Carefully, as the ship righted itself, he worked his way hand over hand to the shelter of the companionway.

There were some crates lashed down against it and he scrambled to squeeze between them and the wall.

The ship heaved again, tilting sharply. Jeremy watched as a wooden bucket that had somehow been left on deck and not tied down skidded down the sloping deck and over the side. It was gone in an instant.

Could have been me, Jeremy thought, shivering as he tried to push his way deeper into the space. It took him a moment to realize there was something, someone, blocking the way.

"Jeremy?" whispered a voice.

He recognized it. He almost said, "Grandad?" but caught himself. Too ridiculous.

"Harv?" He whispered back.

"Squeeze in closer. Looks like we're stuck here until the storm lets up. There's no way we can walk on that deck."

Jeremy squeezed. Somehow there was comfort in being that close together, and cold and soggy as he was now it was good to be able to huddle against someone. Even soaking wet, Harv was a very warm ghost.

"So," Harv began in a much calmer voice than Jeremy thought he could have managed himself, "where's the doorway the stamp takes you to?"

It took Jeremy a minute to figure out what he was getting at.

"I mean," Harv explained, "where do you land when you come on board? It's always the same isn't it? And then you have to go back to that place when you want to be back home. So what's the magic spot on the *Matthew* for you?"

Now Jeremy understood. Forgetting that Harv couldn't see his arm he pointed, "Over there, just by the main mast just below the rigging. Rather dangerous, one of the sailors coming down almost landed on top of me!"

Harv laughed. "I know what you mean, it nearly happened to me once. Every ship's different though. A different way in and out I mean."

This was great! In spite of feeling miserable and cold, this was exactly the kind of conversation he wanted to have.

"You've been on lots of ships!" Jeremy asked eagerly.

"Every stamp I've got!" Harv laughed. "Course that isn't many, I haven't been able to collect very many ship and boat stamps yet! But I like the *Matthew* best. I've sailed with Cabot quite a bit." And then, as the ship gave another mighty lurch, "But not in a storm as bad as this!"

Jeremy shuddered as another wave crashed over the deck. He was admiring Harv's calm. He was still feeling panicky himself.

"Funny though," Harv said in the same even tone, "you and I land in exactly the same place on deck."

Jeremy was curious enough to forget he was nervous. "Why's that funny? I mean, I guess just the fact that we're stamp time-travellers is more than funny-peculiar. It's unbelievable! Never mind where we land on the ships."

Again the reassuring laugh from Harv. Jeremy was really beginning to like him.

"Well, you aren't the first 'ghost' I've run into. There

was someone I met on the 20¢ Cartier stamp once and he came onto the ship in an entirely different place than I did. So I just figured everyone did...I mean had their own spot."

Jeremy knew the answer to that one, at least he thought he did. But if he said, "Maybe it's because we're using the same stamp," he'd have to explain why they were and why he knew they were. So he just said, "Oh." He was starting to feel less scared and more queasy now.

The rolling, pitching motion of the ship didn't seem to be bothering Harv though, although he did sound more thoughtful when he spoke again. "It looks as if we're going to be here awhile." The water from the last wave to wash the deck had even trickled into their hiding place.

Jeremy thought he'd try to sound cheerful and manage a little joke. "At least we know the ship survived the voyage and Cabot got back!"

Harv's answer wasn't what he wanted to hear at all. "I guess so," he said thoughtfully, "unless this is the second voyage."

Harv was right, Jeremy realized uneasily. He remembered what he'd just read in the *World Book.*

The ship seemed to shudder as another wave washed over. How much can a ship tilt until it can't right itself again? Jeremy wondered.

"Some of the books say he was caught in a storm and one ship turned back and nobody heard of Cabot again. So we'd better hope this is the 1497 trip and not the 1498 one."

Wonderful, thought Jeremy. He had to tell me that, didn't he. Now he was feeling queasy *and* scared. He had visions of the ship keeling over and taking on so much water it sank like a stone – with he and Harv jammed in their hideout unable to reach the main mast and get home before it was too late.

The noise of the storm was unbelievable now and the wind seemed to scream in the rigging. He expected to hear one of the masts crack and come smashing onto them. He and Harv were holding on for dear life. If they hadn't been so close together he would not have been able to hear a word Harv was saying.

The thought that this might have been the voyage that sank the *Matthew* was enough to finish him off. What happened to him back at home lying on his bed? In the morning his mother walked in and found a dead boy? Would the autopsy report read, "Died in his sleep of mysterious causes." Obviously, I'm too old to be suspected of crib death.

Wait a minute – the stamp said 1497 so maybe the ship would make it! And there was even more proof than that. Grandad didn't die when he was ten years old. They were going to survive this and get back to their own time.

He would have reached over and patted Harv on the back consolingly if he'd know exactly where to pat, but not wanting to accidentally punch him in the eye, he just said in his most confident voice, "We'll be fine. And the ship won't go down with us on board anyway, we're on the

1497 ship stamp, remember?"

Harv laughed. "Had you going for a minute there, though, didn't I?" He seemed to think a bit. "Anyway I hope you're right. We've got to be positive about it. Worrying won't help, that's for sure."

They sat for awhile in silence. Maybe it was Jeremy's imagination but it seemed that the waves weren't as monstrous and the sea wasn't washing over the deck as much. There hadn't been any water sluicing up to their hiding place for quite a while. Still, he didn't like to say anything in case it was just a temporary calm.

15.

BUT HE HADN'T BEEN WRONG, THE STORM WAS LETTING UP. That was a good thing. Sitting in that cramped space, cold and wet, he was beginning to think he'd never be able to walk again.

Carefully, he eased his way out and stood holding onto the ropes on one of the crates that had formed their shelter. A good thing too, his foot had gone to sleep and wasn't co-operating. The "pins and needles" feeling was starting now and it really hurt.

"The coast is clear!" he whispered to Harv.

After a little fumbling Harv got hold of his hand and managed to get out. He's probably even stiffer than I am, Jeremy thought, he was in there longer and was more scrunched up.

Sailors were starting to move about, almost crablike in the way they did it, moving from hand hold to hand hold on the still rolling ship.

But the sun had come out, piercing the dark clouds.

And on one side of the ship a brilliant rainbow had formed, arcing down into the waves. It seemed so close you could swim out and touch it. Not likely, thought Jeremy, I won't be digging for that pot of gold.

"You okay to head for the mast?" whispered Harv.

Jeremy tested his foot. He could walk now. "Yeah, fine. Watch the deck though, it's still going to be slippery."

They decided to hold hands as they made their way to the place by the mast. That way they wouldn't risk bumping into one another.

IT FELT GOOD TO BE BACK IN HIS BED, though he wished he had an electric blanket to turn on to get the chill out of his bones. The best thing would be to get up and take a hot bath, but that would certainly wake his mother and she'd wonder why he was taking a bath in the middle of the night.

He lay there a bit, listening to the night sounds of the house. There were always some. The furnace fan was on even in the summer because his mother liked to bring cool air up from the basement on hot days. And of course there was the refrigerator. He listened for it to go on. But he heard other sounds. The fridge door, cupboard doors opening and closing, the clink of dishes. What time was it anyway?

The luminous dial on his bedside alarm clock said three o'clock. So what was going on? He crept out of bed and quietly opened his door. Yes, the light was on in the kitchen.

He ducked back just as Aunt Wendy, looking tousled and half asleep came out of the living room and went down the hall to the kitchen. As soon as she went in he followed silently so that he could hear what was going on.

"What's the matter, Sandy?" Aunt Wendy's voice sounded tired. "Can't sleep, huh?"

He could hear his mother blow her nose before she answered. "I thought maybe a cup of herb tea would help me feel better. Remember when we were kids, when we'd had a bad day, we'd ask for chamomile tea because that was what Mrs. Rabbit gave Peter after his bad day in Mr. MacGregor's garden?"

Jeremy recognized his mother's attempt to laugh through tears. It was the way she tried to soften up bad things that happened – by making little jokes that only she found funny.

"Yes," Aunt Wendy sounded really amused. "And it was a good thing too, because nobody would give us real tea when we were that little!"

Then Jeremy could see his mother carrying the tray of tea and cups to the table while Aunt Wendy followed with the milk and sugar. He ducked into the living room doorway to avoid being seen when they sat down. They were moving the chairs very carefully so as not to make any noise as they sat down.

"Oh Wendy, I'm just so worried." His mother's voice

had tears in it. "I can't imagine life without Jeremy. I mean, we've been just the two of us for so long and it's kind of like a team...but part of me knows that I'm being selfish keeping him from having all the advantages that Darrin can give him...." Her voice trailed off. "Anyway, there won't be much option. A court battle will finish me off financially." She blew her nose again.

Aunt Wendy sounded hesitant, "I know you aren't going to like this, but have you talked to Darrin about it?"

Things got very quiet then. He could hear the clinking of a spoon in a teacup as one of them stirred her tea.

"Okay," Aunt Wendy's voice was apologetic. "I'm walking on forbidden ground."

When his mother spoke, Jeremy recognized the tone. It was the one she always used when she was talking about his father and she didn't know he was listening. He called it her "ice cold voice". Once or twice he'd heard it when he'd done something really bad.

"I have *no* intention of talking to *him!*"

Aunt Wendy was being very brave, Jeremy thought, to keep on after that, but she did.

"So how does Jeremy feel about all this? I mean he's the one who's most affected by it. What does he think?"

Thank you, Aunt Wendy!

This time his mother's voice had an altogether different tone. Hesitant, almost apologetic. "Ummm... well...I haven't actually talked to him about it."

It was Aunt Wendy's turn to get loud. "I can't believe it! The poor kid! No wonder he's looking confused and scared."

Jeremy wasn't sure how he should take that. Was he looking confused and scared? He was certainly feeling confused and he would more confused if he hadn't broken the rules and listened to phone calls and eavesdropped the way he was doing now. But was he scared? Maybe.

Maybe that's why he was lurking here in the shadows listening instead of walking in there and taking part in the conversation. After all he had a right to speak for himself, didn't he?"

"Shhhh!" his mother hissed. "You'll wake him."

Jeremy wasn't sure if he'd ever heard Aunt Wendy lose her temper before but she seemed to be doing it now.

"Don't you 'shhh' me, Sandra Thorpe. He *should* wake up. I should go and wake him up. He deserves to get in on this!"

Okay, thought Jeremy, this is like that play they did in school, and now it should say, "Enter Jeremy from the wings, rubbing his eyes sleepily." My cue, he thought. But he didn't move. Maybe he *was* scared. But Aunt Wendy was doing such a good job.

"He's not just a piece of furniture you two can pass back and forth...think about how he must feel!"

Jeremy was feeling very like a piece of furniture just then. Something that got stuck in the doorway and couldn't move.

He didn't want to get mixed up in this. But Aunt Wendy was right, he had to tell them how he felt.

Now his mother was sobbing and Aunt Wendy was apologizing. He realized he could probably just sneak back to bed and stay out of it. No, that would be admitting he was chicken – like the time Charlie'd dared him to walk the roof beam of the garage. He'd done it rather than admit the fear. Pretty dumb, he could have been killed.

This time he wouldn't be admitting it to anybody but himself. But he wasn't chicken. He'd been really brave with Harv when he thought the *Matthew* was going to sink. Quickly, before he could change his mind, he stopped being a piece of furniture and walked down the hall to the kitchen.

His mother looked up teary-eyed, "I'm sorry Jer-Bear, did we wake you?"

"No," he said. His voice was wobbly but he kept the words firm, "I was awake and I heard you making tea."

"And everything else, I suppose," his mother sniffled.

"And everything else," said Jeremy and this time his voice was firm too.

16.

NOBODY SAID ANYTHING FOR A MINUTE. HE HADN'T known the kitchen clock had such a loud tick.

Of course it was Aunt Wendy who spoke first. Her voice was soft. "Tell him, Sandra."

Then his mother began to talk. All about the day she got the forms asking for a custody hearing.

"That's all?" asked Aunt Wendy. She obviously hadn't heard it all yet, either. "I mean, what did he say when you talked to him about more support?"

Jeremy waited. He wondered if his dad had asked about him. But his mother wouldn't say anything about that, he knew. He used to hang around when the letters came in with the cheque each month, for awhile he'd dug them out of the wastepaper basket looking for a note, but he'd given that up years ago.

His mother concentrated on pouring herself another cup of tea, adding sugar and stirring. Finally she said, "I didn't talk to him," her voice was muffled by the tea cup at her lips. "I went to Legal Aid and had them send a letter."

Aunt Wendy groaned, but she didn't say anything.

Jeremy was beginning to wish that he had snuck back to bed, but it was too late. Aunt Wendy had turned to him, "So what about you, kiddo? How do you feel about all this?"

How did he feel? For one thing, he hated the lump in his stomach just now. Maybe he just wasn't at his best at three o'clock in the morning. And he hadn't quite figured out how he felt.

He did want to see his dad. Other kids of divorced parents got to spend time with their dads.

And he was curious. His dad had moved East when he left, but Jeremy didn't even know where he lived. The cheque letters all came from his office, and that was in Toronto, but did he have a house in a suburb or did he live in a condo downtown? He'd never even met his dad's new wife. Not exactly "new" either, they'd been married for nearly six years, longer, he realized, than his mother and father had been together.

The knot in his stomach was tightening, like somebody pulling the strings. And he was taking much too long with this answer. His mother was starting to look even more upset.

He cleared his throat. "I...I don't want to leave Mum," he said slowly, "but I'd like to visit dad sometime." His voice trailed off. "I don't even know him...but maybe a short visit."

His mother's face had brightened at first but with the last bit it clouded up again. Oh-oh, thought Jeremy, I've done it now. He'd been sort of thinking out loud and hadn't prepared himself for this. Why on earth hadn't he stayed on the *Matthew*? It was more fun even in a life-threatening storm, especially with Harv there.

Once again Aunt Wendy came to his rescue. She got up, got a cup, and poured him a bit of tea. "If it's good enough for Peter Rabbit," she said, giving his shoulder a squeeze, "it's good enough for you!"

They went to bed then. He was sure he couldn't sleep. In fact, he planned to wait a bit until they'd all settled down and then use his flashlight to look at the stamp again.

He didn't make it. The next thing he knew there was sunlight streaming through his window.

It took him a little while to realize how late it was. Mum would have left for work quite awhile ago. Usually she'd come in and wake him to say goodbye before she left so that he wouldn't waste his whole summer holiday in bed, she said.

Maybe she'd let him sleep because he'd been up so late last night. Maybe she'd slept in and been in too much of a hurry. He didn't like to think of the last possibility – that she was mad at him for wanting to visit Dad.

Dad. Funny. He realized he hadn't ever actually called his father that to his face. He'd still been calling him "Daddy" when he left. That was what four-year-olds usually did.

He listened but couldn't hear anything but the usual

house sounds. Where was Aunt Wendy? Still asleep? If she was he could grab the stamp book and see if he could find Harv again.

He tiptoed out of his room and peeked into the living room.

The comforter she was using was folded neatly on the couch beside her pillow. He wandered from room to room. It didn't take long in such a small house. He even knocked gently on his mother's door and after waiting a minute peeked in, just in case Aunt Wendy had decided to crawl into the big double bed. After all it must be uncomfortable on the couch. Maybe he should volunteer to trade beds with her. Why hadn't his mother suggested it?

HE'D JUST DECIDED IT WAS SAFE to go back to bed when Aunt Wendy burst through the front door.

"Aha! Up at last are you? You're a real slug-a-bed today." She stopped and seemed to wilt. "Maybe I should have done the same thing," she yawned. "Your mother's middle-of-the-night tea party was a bit much!"

Jeremy laughed. "Right!" he said. "If it had been the Mad Hatter's tea party, I'd have wanted to be the dormouse and get some sleep!"

"Dormouse?" smiled Aunt Wendy. "Your mother was so upset we're lucky *both* of us didn't get stuffed in the teapot!"

He was grateful to Aunt Wendy for keeping it light.

He didn't like serious talks in the middle of the night, he'd discovered. Come to think of it, he wasn't very fond of serious talks at the best of times.

"I thought I'd catch a ride downtown with your mother and get a couple of things." Aunt Wendy was pulling something out of a plastic bag. "This is for you!"

Not more school clothes! Jeremy wondered how he could stand any more trying on. But it wasn't clothes at all. It was a book with spiral binding. A diary? Jeremy wondered. She doesn't really expect me to keep a diary. But it wasn't that either.

Stamps of Canada Catalogue, he read. He flipped the pages. There were pictures of all the stamps ever printed in Canada by the look of it.

What was he supposed to do with this? He wasn't a collector. And Grandad's collection was so small. It didn't make sense. He was sorry Aunt Wendy seemed so excited about it. Now he'd have to pretend to be too. And not knowing why made it hard to do.

17.

JEREMY FIGURED SAYING, "WOW! A STAMP CATALOGUE! Just what I've always wanted!" would be carrying it a bit far. So he let his voice show some of his puzzlement and just a touch of pleasure.

"A stamp catalogue?" he said. And waited, hoping Aunt Wendy would explain why this was supposed to be a neat gift.

She did. "I figured you could look up some of those stamps you've got," she said as she carried a few groceries she'd bought into the kitchen.

Right, thought Jeremy, not sure why he needed to do that. He leafed through the book. He supposed he could find out what year some of the stamps were issued, though most of them already had it printed on if they were commemorating a voyage of some kind.

So he didn't need the dates and he didn't care about the designers or engravers who were listed. He looked at the lists beneath the pictures. N1, N2, U, FDC – what did that mean? But there were dollar signs and amounts and it suddenly dawned on him. Of course! Even used stamps were worth money if they were old enough. He'd forgotten that. And if some of the stamps were worth enough, he'd be helping his mother way more than just by getting a part time job.

He hurried to his room and started checking out some of the stamps.

Half-an-hour later, when Aunt Wendy called him for breakfast, which was really brunch since it was so late now, he'd learned that N1 meant "new 1st quality", N2 was "new 2nd quality" – which seemed to mean that the borders weren't quite perfect, U was used, and FDC meant an envelope with the stamp on it cancelled and stood for "First Day Cover."

He'd checked a few of the stamps and the biggest amount he'd come up with so far would have been the *Nonsuch*. That is, if it was a variation one with a "big wave." That one would be worth $5.00 new or $2.50 used.

Since all of Grandad's stamps were cancelled they fell in the U category. He wasn't even sure if it was the "big wave" variety. He really couldn't see much difference. If it wasn't it was only worth ten cents.

At least he knew now why Aunt Wendy had got him the catalogue, so when he plopped himself down at the table he knew what she meant when she asked, "Any luck?"

"No," he said dejectedly. He perked up considerably when she set the plate of bacon, eggs, hash browns and sliced tomato in front of him. "But I haven't checked all the stamps yet." He let a little optimism creep into his voice. Food always cheered him up.

Luckily he finished eating before it crossed his mind that since the *Matthew* was an older stamp it might be worth more. What if it was worth hundreds? He'd have to give it up and maybe he'd never see Harv again.

The thought made his stomach knot up. Not an easy thing to do when it was so full of food. Without meaning to, he groaned.

Instantly, Aunt Wendy was at his side.

"What's the matter, kiddo?" She was all concern.

Jeremy was sorry about the groan. "I'm okay...really. Just ate too fast, I guess."

Aunt Wendy laughed. "Too fast and too much! I've never seen anybody who could pack food away like you do!"

"I'll just lie down for a bit, I think." He said. Actually this could work out fine.

He wasn't even going to look at the *Matthew* in the stamp catalogue until he'd had at least one more visit. Now, more than ever, he wished that he'd arranged a meeting place with Harv.

The chances of them bumping into each other three times in a row were very slim. Unless Harv spent half his time on the ship.

JEREMY LANDED NEXT TO THE MAST and checked carefully around to make sure he wouldn't bump into anybody. All clear. Nobody up the mast and no sailors nearby.

The day was clear with a brisk wind filling the sails above him. Thank goodness the storm was over. He walked towards the aft rail swaying a bit for balance.

The closest person he could see was Bart, who was behind him near the companionway where he and Harv had hidden before. He could risk calling. He figured his voice would be carried away by the wind and if not, one more of Bart's "ghost" stories wouldn't make much difference to the crew.

"Harv!" He called. "Harv?"

Give up, he thought to himself. He's got a life, he can't be spending all his time on the stamps. Jeremy slumped dejectedly against the rail. It was stupid to think that they'd meet again, even if they did both use the same stamp.

"Harv!" This time he didn't even call, just said the name to himself.

But somewhere behind him he heard a voice answering.

"Jeremy?" said the voice. "Where are you? Keep talking"

He spun around. He couldn't believe it! "Over here!" he called forgetting to even worry about the noise. "By the big coil of rope!"

He could hear Harv laughing, coming closer. "That's a big help," he was saying, "only about seventy coils of rope aboard!" Then he felt Harv moving beside him holding onto the rail.

Jeremy was overjoyed. "I can't believe it! I never expected to find you again. Do you spend all your time on this stamp?"

Harv laughed, "Yeah, I have been here a lot. I knew you'd come back sometime, so I've been checking as often as I could. I think Mother is getting worried about me."

A scene flashed before Jeremy's eyes. He remembered his visit to Great-Granny Stark in the nursing home in Prince Albert. She'd been mixed up, thinking Jeremy was her son.

"You're spending too much time with those stamps..." she'd said. "All day you're in the room with that magnifying glass and those stamps...."

Jeremy'd been confused at the time. But she just had the wrong boy. Jeremy wasn't her son but Harv was.

This might have been the very time that she'd been rambling on about, the time her son spent so much time with the stamps.

He felt a poke. "You still there? Thought maybe you'd fallen overboard. You're so quiet."

"Just thinking..."

But Harv's attention was caught by some activity behind them on the foredeck. "Say they're going to land soon. Look!"

18.

JEREMY HADN'T EVEN NOTICED THE LAND AHEAD BUT the wind was bringing them in towards a harbour. Now it seemed the decks were alive with sailors. Sails were being lowered. All hands were busy. The sounds of creaking masts and snapping sails filled the air.

"C'mon," said Harv as he grabbed Jeremy's hand from the railing, "Let's see if we can find a spot on the fore-deck. I want to see this!"

"I looked this up," whispered Harv as they moved along. "Apparently they missed England altogether and are about to land in France!"

Jeremy laughed, "So Cabot and his 'astrolabe' weren't wrong, after all!" He started to explain the argument he'd witnessed but Harv interrupted him.

"I was there too, remember? That was the first time we 'bumped' into each other!"

Carefully they moved through the melee of ropes and sailors to climb up to the foredeck. Jeremy'd only been up here once before when they were landing in Newfoundland. Now he was going to be in on the return.

Huddled together in a corner by the rail, they watched as the ship entered the harbour at Brittany.

There was excitement and confusion aboard the ship. It didn't take long for the crew to realize that they'd missed their intended landfall.

"We've missed Bristol channel," mumbled one of the men nearby.

Cabot was smiling triumphantly. The other officers didn't look so happy. "It will take three days to get back to Bristol," someone announced.

Jeremy thought Cabot was being quite good-natured about having his triumphant return delayed.

He felt Harv pulling him along. Of course, they'd have to look sharp and get out of the way before the men started going ashore.

"I'm going to go on another stamp tomorrow," Harv whispered. "Let's meet by the aft rail on the port side of the *Bluenose*."

Jeremy could hear the excitement in his voice. He really did love the stamp ships. He just hoped they wouldn't get caught in a storm again. He just had time to say "yes" before he felt Harv's hand pulled away as he "whooshed" back in time.

Moments later Jeremy was back too. Lying on his bed. Aunt Wendy was just headed out the door. She turned to pull it shut and saw him watching.

"Sorry," she whispered. "I didn't know you were asleep. Did I wake you? I just brought you a glass of water."

It was there on the bedside table. He hadn't heard a thing. He decided it was a good thing he'd been lying down with the book.

He waited until she'd closed the door and then got the catalogue. He was brave enough to look up the *Matthew* stamp now.

Ten cents! It was only worth ten cents! He felt himself being torn between sad and glad. Glad was definitely winning. He wouldn't have to give up the stamp! But he wasn't going to be able to hand his mother a nice bundle of money either.

And he wanted to get some money. He was sure that this whole fight wasn't over him at all. It was over money, and if his mother backed off, his dad would too. That was how Aunt Wendy felt too, he was pretty sure.

He tried not to think of how that made him feel. Knowing that his dad probably hadn't really wanted Jeremy to come and live with him. Were his parents really doing this just to spite each other?

He knew his mother really needed the money. He hated seeing her so depressed. It was actually worse at the end of the month when she got paid and realized that there wasn't going to be enough to pay everything.

But maybe Aunt Wendy was right. Why hadn't she just asked? It would have been nicer, wouldn't it? Nicer for his dad than getting a letter from a lawyer.

His mother had never forgiven his father. The resentment was still there, he'd seen it the night she was talking to Aunt Wendy. So she'd never spoken to dad for over six years. Never even written a letter.

His dad probably didn't even know what he looked like. No school pictures or Christmas cards or anything to let him know.

He wondered if some of this was his own fault. Every time he mentioned his dad, and when he was little he remembered doing it a lot, his mother got so angry or upset that it just seemed smarter not to say a word. How many years had it been since he'd even tried?

Okay. Maybe he should try. He had the sinking feeling that his mother would think he was a traitor if he wrote to Dad but he did have an excuse. The computer. After all it was only polite to say "thank you" wasn't it?

He sat down. What was the program that you used for writing things? Aunt Wendy had showed him. There it was, "Word Pro". He wished he'd paid more attention when Aunt Wendy was giving instructions. Oh well, he'd figure it out.

Dear Dad, he wrote. What now? *Remember me? I am your son, Jeremy?* No, too corny. Dad would know who it was. He could always look at the signature. How many Jeremys did he have calling him "Dad" anyway?

Thank you for the computer. The guys at the computer store put all kinds of neat stuff on it for me – encyclopedia and some great games – I guess you told them to do that. Thanks. I never thought I'd be lucky enough to have a computer of my own.

Now what? He sat staring at the computer screen. What do I say? "Mum and I are very poor so please increase the support payments and don't go to Court because she can't afford that and I know you don't really want me to live with you but I'd like to see you some time?"

He grinned in spite of himself. Not likely! That sounded pretty pathetic. He stared at the computer screen a bit more and then typed, *My phone number is 433-6878 if you ever want to phone me and talk.*

That's enough, he decided. I just have to sign off. *Sincerely, your son, Jeremy.* No, that was too formal. He backspaced and erased it all, stared awhile longer and then typed; *Love, Jeremy.*

It was easy to save it, it took him a little longer figuring out how to put it on a disk. He almost thought he was going to have to call Aunt Wendy for help but he finally figured it out.

Tomorrow Charlie was back and then he could see about getting it printed.

It wasn't until later that he realized he didn't know his dad's address.

19.

CHARLIE WAS BACK.

Ordinarily that would have been cause for celebration, even though it meant that there were only a few more days until school started. This time, Jeremy thought, as he walked the three blocks it took to get to Charlie's, he wasn't even sure he wanted to see his friend.

Charlie would be full of news about the trip he'd taken with his parents to Vancouver Island, all the things he'd seen and done on Long Beach or whale watching at Tofino. He'd managed to get that much in just in a short phone call.

What did Jeremy have to tell? I'm in the midst of a custody battle and don't know where I'll be living?

Actually he had done some travelling himself. But he could hardly say, "You may have ridden the Vancouver Island ferry but I discovered North America with John Cabot!"

He'd never dared tell Charlie about his time-travelling with the stamps. Oh, he'd given it a lot of thought, but how do you tell somebody that?

"Hi, I just went back over five hundred years by looking at a stamp picture of an olden days sailing ship?" Charlie wouldn't believe him and he couldn't prove it. After all his body stayed right there on the bed. Charlie'd just think he was faking it and be mad.

He was almost sorry that he'd agreed to come over to Charlie's anyway. He should be at home seeing if he could meet up with Harv on the *Bluenose* stamp. He could have used the excuse that Aunt Wendy was leaving in a day or two. Except that wasn't a very good excuse. After all, he and Charlie only had a few days to celebrate summer holidays. He felt the disk in its plastic case in his pocket. A reason to be here. At least he'd get the letter printed.

Charlie was waiting on his front step.

"Took you long enough!" Charlie said, but he was grinning as they went inside. "Wait 'til you see all the neat stuff I found beachcombing!"

Jeremy had to admit that Charlie'd found some great driftwood, some clamshells and a lot of coloured bits of glass that had been worn smooth by the sea. Charlie'd decided to arrange these in a collage picture but he hadn't figured out what it would be.

"And we saw a pod of orcas!"

Charlie pulled out an envelope of snapshots that turned out to be disappointing. It seemed the whales knew exactly when Charlie was going to snap the picture and decided to dive, though there were some convincing splashes and one or two blurs that might have been whale flukes.

Jeremy decided that Charlie's future didn't lie in nature photography but he didn't say anything. He could tell Charlie was thrilled by it all and he didn't want to rain on his parade.

He waited for the next words: "What did you do all summer?" He didn't want to hear them so he jumped in quickly before Charlie could ask.

"Can you print this for me?" Jeremy pulled the disk from his pocket. "My dad sent me a computer but I haven't got a printer so I can't print anything yet."

Charlie was obviously impressed. He'd actually stopped with his mouth open about to say something.

"Wow!" was all he could say.

Then Jeremy realized that it wasn't the computer that had impressed Charlie.

"Your dad sent you something?"

Charlie's tone was awe struck. It actually made Jeremy laugh. Anybody else acting like that would have hurt his feelings but he knew that Charlie knew how much Jeremy missed having any contact with his father. Charlie understood.

Jeremy decided to be cool. "Yeah. And he wants me to go and live with him."

Charlie's reaction was even better than he'd expected. Amazement and dismay seemed to be fighting for centre stage on his face. The dismay won. "You're not going to be moving away?" Charlie was crestfallen.

Jeremy felt a little guilty. In just a few seconds it seemed that Charlie had given more thought to the possibility of Jeremy actually moving away for good than he had himself. It just hadn't seemed real to him. All he'd been thinking about was the upset of a custody fight and how angry and miserable his mother had been feeling. Not the actual fact of not being here any more. He'd really only brought the whole thing up to distract Charlie from bragging about his vacation and because he didn't want to admit that he hadn't had a real holiday.

Now he was sorry. Part of the fun of having a great holiday was probably being able to relive it when you told someone about it. He'd rained on Charlie's parade after all.

"I don't think it will happen..." he said hoping to cheer Charlie up. "My mum's going to fight it and I don't want to go." He decided to change the subject. "So, what did you bring me?"

They always bought each other the tackiest souvenir they could find. Last year when Jeremy had visited P.A. with his mother to see Great-granny Stark, he'd found a mangy-looking bear key chain with Souvenir of Waskesiu on it.

It worked. Charlie looked much more cheerful, reached in his pocket and produced a snow globe with two orcas leaping through the blizzard. Charlie always bought snow globes for him. Jeremy now had four, including a Mountie on horseback from Regina and Jasper the bear. The other was a bucking bronco from Calgary with the cowboy falling off in the storm.

"Hey, can you stay for supper?"

Jeremy didn't really want to, Aunt Wendy was leaving to go back to Saskatchewan day after tomorrow and he wanted to get onto the *Bluenose* again. On the other hand it was great seeing Charlie after all this time.

"I'll have to phone home and see," was the way he solved it. He'd let his mother decide. "Meanwhile, let's print this letter to my dad."

Supper was good. Mrs. Welles made great lasagna. When all the talk of the trip and Charlie's adventures with the whales was over and everyone was leaving the table, Charlie's dad turned to Jeremy.

"And how's my young friend doing? Any more history projects?"

Jeremy knew it was really a joke. Mr. Welles taught History and had helped him last year when he was doing a school project on the voyage of the *Nonsuch*. Jeremy knew he could have mumbled something like, "Fine, thanks" and kept going. But he wasn't about to let a chance like this get away.

"I've been very interested in John Cabot," he said seriously. "Where he landed with the *Matthew* in 1497." He waited.

Mr. Welles looked pleased. "Even without a school

project you are interested in Canadian history, are you? Well, my boy, you've picked a subject that has fascinated a lot of people."

They were in Mr. Welles' study now, standing before a map. Jeremy noticed that Charlie was standing impatiently by the door. Mr. Welles ignored him and pointed to a map of Canada.

"The big mystery is whether he landed here in Cape Breton Island, up here in one of the capes of Newfoundland or missed both and hit Labrador."

"Hey, this isn't a Social Studies class!" Charlie interrupted. "C'mon Jeremy!"

Charlie's father ignored him. "It would be wonderful to know just exactly where he planted the flag."

"Two flags," Jeremy corrected without thinking. Now he could find out something he'd wondered about. "Why two?"

Mr. Welles looked a bit shocked but Jeremy could tell he was pleased. "I'm impressed, young man. You are right. There were supposedly two. One was the banner of his patron, Henry VII of England. The Cross of St. George, a red cross on a white background. The other was the flag of Venice. After all Cabot or Caboto was a citizen of Venice at the time."

Jeremy nodded. "So that's it," he said, almost to himself, "the lion with wings, standing on his hind legs with his foot on a book was Venice..."

Charlie had by now grabbed Jeremy by the arm. "You

promised your mum you'd be home by seven," he said.

It was a good thing Charlie was pulling him out of the door. Mr. Welles' expression as he looked after Jeremy was more than just puzzled. He looked thunderstuck.

20.

JEREMY LAY IN BED THAT NIGHT STARING AT THE STAMP of the *Bluenose*. Twice he'd gone back and there had been no sign of Harv. If he hadn't known that Harv had grown up to be his Grandad he'd have started to suspect something awful had happened to him.

The stamp of the beautiful schooner, its sails bent to the wind, with its first captain Angus Walters in the background stared back at him.

Suddenly it dawned on him. There was more than one stamp of the *Bluenose!* As a matter of fact, there was more than one *Bluenose!*

Of course. The stamp was too recent for Grandad to have been on it. He needed an old stamp. A stamp of the first *Bluenose*.

He couldn't turn the pages quickly enough. There it was, the old 50¢ *Bluenose* stamp. It was even older than the *Matthew* stamp. He grabbed the stamp catalogue. The stamp in Grandad's album was badly marked and even torn a little. Definitely "used". But this was the best yet. $60.00. Wow! And if it was one of the ones the catalogue called the "man in the mast" variety it would be worth fifteen hundred dollars! Now that would cheer his mother up.

That gave Jeremy an idea. He picked up the magnifying glass. He couldn't wait to see Harv.

Why, he wondered as he clung to the mast, did he always have to hit the deck on these stamps in the middle of a storm? The *Bluenose* was keeling over. There was nothing to do but move back into position and hope that he wouldn't be swept away by the gale force winds before he got safely back home.

He lay there in bed hoping Harv had managed to get safely away as well. How long would he have to wait to go back and miss the storm? Time didn't work the same, though he'd noticed that he never went back to a time earlier than his previous visit to the ships. To kill a bit of time he got out the stamp catalogue and made a list of stamps.

This time when he arrived back the storm was over. But it evidently hadn't been over long. The deck looked as if a bomb had hit. Above him shredded sails flapped in the breeze. One mast had been torn loose with all the rigging and booms scattered or gone overboard. Two lifeboats dangled uselessly, smashed beyond repair.

"Wow!" he breathed forgetting to check if he was alone.

"Wow is right!" came Harv's voice nearby.

"I hope you weren't caught in this?" Jeremy asked. "I showed up just as she was keeling over and got away."

"I wasn't so lucky," Harv said ruefully. "I'd headed for the galley to get some shelter before it got really bad. Then I couldn't get back. And the galley broke loose from its housing so that was pretty scary. I'd have thought I was a goner if I hadn't realize this was the famous storm the *Bluenose* got caught in on the way back from England in 1936."

"You're smart to read about the ships *before* you go on them," Jeremy said. "I always end up looking things up afterwards! I'd have been *sure* I was a goner!" But I'd have known you'd survive, he thought, smiling to himself.

They found themselves a spot out of the way and huddled out of the wind which still blew fresh and cool enough to make Jeremy's eyes water.

At last a chance to talk. Jeremy told Harv why he hadn't made it sooner because of looking at the wrong stamp.

"I had a problem too," Harv said and his voice was sad. "Mother thinks I spend too much time over the stamps. She's threatening to take my stamp album away for awhile."

That was something Jeremy hadn't figured on. He still hadn't told Harv the important thing he wanted. "Oh no..." he groaned. "Just when I wanted to get you to do me a favour."

Harv was such a nice guy. All he said was, "Sure, what can I do?"

Jeremy explained. And then he started telling Harv about the stamps. The ones that would become valuable later on.

"Even if I can't get back on any ships for awhile, I can do that." He said slowly, "and you say the ones with a capital *G* on them are better to collect?"

"Yeah, and ones that haven't been used are the best, if you can afford to keep those." Jeremy was amazed that Harv hadn't asked why Jeremy was asking for this. Not even when they started talking about hiding the stamps in a special place. Harv just seemed to like the idea of secret hiding places.

At last they shook hands to leave. Both were trying hard not to laugh out loud. It was hard finding someone's hand when you couldn't see it or your own.

Back in his bed, Jeremy turned out the light and went to sleep, smiling.

21.

THE STAMP SHOP WAS IN A BASEMENT ON WHYTE AVENUE.

It was the second one Jeremy had been to. He'd been at West Eddy Mall with Charlie yesterday and had walked in to look around. He figured he'd come back alone if it looked like a place where he'd feel comfortable asking questions. But there were so many people and the guy behind the counter was busy, so he'd just leafed through the book of stamps on the counter. Most of his stamps weren't there. He took that as a good sign. Maybe they really were valuable and the owner didn't want them out where they might be stolen.

This place was different. It was kind of cluttered and comfortable and just now it was empty.

The old man behind the counter looked politely bored when Jeremy pulled out the stamp book. None of the ship stamps seemed to interest him but he smiled at Jeremy in a friendly way.

"It's good to see a young fellow like you so interested

in collecting," he said. "Sometimes I'm afraid it's turned into an old man's hobby." He sighed then, looked at Jeremy again and laughed. "Maybe I shouldn't have said that. You might not want to be doing it!"

Jeremy felt much braver now. Nothing ventured – nothing gained, his mother said was Grandad's favourite saying. Taking a deep breath, he pulled off the top of the page Harv had said he would glue to the back cover.

He hadn't dared look before, though he knew there was something there.

Inside were dozens of loose stamps. Even Jeremy was amazed. The man at the stamp shop started flipping them over and suddenly he was no longer bored.

"Do you have any idea how much these are worth, kid?"

It surprised him that he didn't mind being called kid. Somehow it sounded warm, like Aunt Wendy's "kiddo."

He pulled the stamp catalogue out and flipped it open. The stamps he'd marked to tell Harv to buy were not only lying there on the table, there were several of each of them.

"Yeah," he said, "...sort of."

The man didn't seem to be listening. He'd brought over his calculator and his fingers were flying over the keys as he sorted the stamps neatly into piles.

"Tell you what," he said finally when he stopped. "You sell me these and I'll give you a hint about these."

He'd separated out about six stamps which he pushed towards Jeremy.

"How much?" Jeremy asked. "For the others, I mean."

The man laughed. Jeremy decided he was not a bad guy. He liked the way his face crinkled up when he laughed. There were more lines around his eyes from laughing than centre creases in his forehead from frowning. Jeremy liked that. He thought it was kind of grandfatherly.

"I'll have to make a list and check them out but I think you're looking at nearly five thousand dollars here."

Jeremy's mouth dropped open. The man smiled kindly and went on talking.

"I don't think you should wander around with that kind of cash so I can give you a money order or a cheque if you bring them back tomorrow. That is if you want to sell them to me." There was a twinkle in the man's eye.

Jeremy nodded dumbly.

"And these," the man went on pointing to the other stamps, "would probably make more at auction on the Internet. I could help you with that if you like."

Jeremy was still nodding but now he had a big dumb grin on his face.

"You know," the man was saying as he looked at Jeremy. "If you aren't busy Saturday afternoons I could use a fellow around the store...somebody with a proper respect for stamps...to help out and sort things when I get busy."

He was looking at Jeremy with an amused expression. Jeremy realized that he probably looked like one of those bobbing head drinking bird toys and stopped nodding. But he couldn't wipe the grin off and what's more he didn't want to.

"Yes, Sir!" was all he could think of to say.

"Matthews. Mr. Matthews," the man said holding out his hand to shake Jeremy's.

It had been a bit of a blur after that. Somehow he made it home.

It had been all he could do not to say anything to his mother.

22.

TODAY WAS TURNING OUT TO BE A DAY IN A MILLION.

First of all, he was very pleased with himself about solving the problem of Dad's address. Super Sleuth had simply waited for the support cheque to show up, fished the envelope out of the wastepaper basket where his mother had pitched it, and used the office address.

Today, there it was, a letter for him, in the mailbox. He hadn't expected a reply so quickly. His dad must have written right back.

He folded the letter and put it back in the envelope. He'd save it awhile and then show it to his mother. Right now he just wanted to savour the feeling of having something private.

He walked to the stamp store, eagerly at first and then getting slower and slower thinking that maybe it had all been a dream and the nice old man wouldn't be there and there wouldn't be any five thousand dollars or a Saturday job.

Was the man's name really Matthews? He hadn't

made the connection with the ship before. Either Matthew was a very lucky name for him or it really was just a dream.

But the store was still there at the foot of the stairs and so was Mr. Matthews who smiled and said, "Now, let's see those stamps again."

Jeremy smiled back and dumped them out of the pocket in the back of the album.

For awhile neither of them said anything. Mr. Matthews went over his list making tiny check marks after each one and adding on his calculator again.

And now Jeremy not only had a letter from his Dad, he had a cheque for $4,267.00 in his pocket to give to his mother.

He hoped that she'd start complaining about the bills and getting the car fixed or something and then he could pull it out of his pocket and say, "Will this help?" He'd try to look innocent and not to grin so that she wouldn't suspect anything. He couldn't wait to see the look on her face.

EVERYTHING WENT THE WAY HE'D PLANNED. Even better maybe. His mother had laughed and cried and hugged him and then done it all over again. He felt like a Superhero, saving the day.

He lay in bed that night feeling as if things couldn't possibly get better. He hadn't even told his mother yet about the letter from dad and that there would be no custody battle. At least if Jeremy could just get them to talk about visiting once in a while.

He knew that wouldn't be easy. Maybe impossible. He'd heard stories of kids at school whose divorced parents tried to get even by making things difficult for each other. It seemed to him it was the kid who got hurt the most.

There was Bryan in his grade, who never knew which parent he'd be spending Christmas with because they were always fighting about it. One year they'd even gone to court just over that. Bryan was miserable most of the time but he didn't let anyone sympathize with him. In fact he was turning into the class bully.

And then there was Melissa. Jeremy wouldn't even have known that she had a problem, if he hadn't seen her crying on the way to school. Mostly though, she just tried to be perfect and threw up a lot.

So maybe he couldn't solve his parents' battle. But he'd be braver about letting Mum know how he felt.

And he had money and a job and he still had those six stamps.

He switched on the bedside light and looked at the album in his lap. Flipping it open to the back cover he felt in the pocket for them. One seemed to be stuck at the bottom, so he ripped the pocket off completely. He could scotch tape it back again.

And then he realized the back page was covered in

writing. Pencil writing that hadn't shown through. It was a letter to him and it was signed "Grandad (Harv)."

Dear Jeremy,

It was great spending time with you on the Matthew *and the* Bluenose – *even the storms! I'm so glad I got to know you, you make a great friend. Here are all the stamps I could find for you. Some were pretty expensive already when I tried to get them as a kid but I kept buying whenever I had a bit of extra money. The last two I actually got after you were born. By the way, I didn't realize who you were for quite awhile. I wish I could have been around to talk to you after you made those trips and met Harv, but time isn't always on our side. Still, I'm thankful we got the better of time for a little while because of the stamps.*

Love, Grandad (Harv).

He turned out the light and remembered.

ACKNOWLEDGEMENTS

The author would like to acknowledge the following people who helped in the writing and preparation of this book: Harrison Taylor for his expertise in computers and games boys like to play, Fred Kerner for his advice on stamps and collecting, Eleanor McEachern for reading the manuscript, and Earl Georgas for reading the manuscript and everything else!

AUTHOR PHOTO BY BENJE BONDAR

ABOUT THE AUTHOR

One of Canada's best-known children's authors, Cora Taylor has published seven juvenile novels, including the award-winning *Julie, Julie's Secret, The Doll,* and *Summer of the Mad Monk.* Her most recent novel is *On Wings of a Dragon.* She has received numerous awards and commendations for her work, and has served in writer in residence positions from St. Albert, Alberta, to Tasmania.

Cora Taylor was born in Fort Qu'Appelle, Saskatchewan, and grew up on a farm near Fort Carlton. After moving to Alberta, she studied writing with W.O. Mitchell and Rudy Wiebe, and published her first book, *Julie*, in 1985. She continues to live and write in Edmonton.